I0715727

Memorial Club

Memorial Club

A Novel

MOZID MAHMUD

First English edition published by Gaudy Boy. Previously published in Bangla by Mozid Mahmud in slightly altered form in 2020.

Published by Gaudy Boy LLC,
an imprint of Singapore Unbound
www.singaporeunbound.org/gaudyboy
New York

For more information on ordering books, contact jkoh@singaporeunbound.org.

ISBN 978-1-958652-16-9
eISBN 978-1-958652-15-2

Library of Congress Control Number: 2024939677

Cover design by Flora Chan
Interior design by Jennifer Houle

For Abdul Wahab Biswas, my eldest brother

*An author of many stories and poems, none of which survived
the mites in his trunk apart from the poem, "Mala"*

The Trial

Months later when Hasan finds himself at the rehabilitation center in Shyamoli, he will remember this dream: Seeing a manhole. Hospital grounds. Beyond it a vast field. The grass's green blades with dew on their tips. He has a potli bag on his head. Chomir's breakfast, khichuri with the husk of the lentil still intact, onions and red chilies. With the food in his arms, he crosses the fields, where his eyes fall to the unending white of catkin. Hasan feels a rumble inside him as he travels past the green and into the white saree-like embrace of the swaying young buds. Chomir walks up to the river with a wooden plow. Indentured for a year as a farmer to Hasan's family, he will tie the cows to the yoke and sit down to eat. His one morsel will assuage half of Hasan's hunger. A river flows from the raked crevices of the field, a river named Padma. In the paddy field on one side of the river, a girl is moving toward him. She looks like Morzina. He hasn't seen her in a long while. She looks the same age as before. The girl, seeing him, has turned her back and is heading the opposite way, toward the river. An illusion, perhaps. The girl is not Morzina. Dragging the plow with her toward the river, she looks back at him and then walks away. She does this the way Bilu did—is she Bilu? Hasan's body jerks in pain. He wonders if Chomir is coming this way. Failing on all fronts to control himself, he wakes up as if he has had a seizure.

A sliver of Falgun's late-evening light melts through the window and falls over Hasan's eyes. He wakes up. He is alone, he feels alone. All the nonsense he sees in his dreams! In each cell of his body, he feels torment building up. The pain brims over. The last light of the day melts away Hasan's exhaustions, especially from the dream he just had.

Fariha isn't home. She has gone to visit her parents. He lies in bed, his legs straight. There's little energy left in him. Fariha will soon be a mother. The prospect of fatherhood leaves him unnerved. He feels like he is too young for it. He is in his thirties. He graduated from university a while ago. His father died recently. Hasan's good university results and his job don't provide him with any pleasure. His marriage, which took place too quickly, does not either, much to his chagrin.

His mood worsens as he remembers the dream he just had. One night in 1978, a little more than two decades ago. A swampy, grimy little village with a river wriggling down it like one's private parts between one's legs. A river where Hasan learned how to swim in his childhood. Today this river is dying. It dries up naked with the first murmur of winter. Hasan must have learned how to swim like the freshwater insects. The diving, the floating on your back, the going away somewhere and touching other things within the water—who had taught him this? Morzina or Chomir or perhaps even the family's brownish cow?

Morzina had said, "If you don't know how to swim, how will you catch me?" She used to live on the other side of the river. Their tin-shed house, facing south, had a palm tree beside it. The tall tree was a source of pride for the village, especially for Hasan during his adolescence. Only in this regard was Morzina able to differentiate herself from him. They were both similar as students, had the same likes and played the same games. Everyone knew Morzina as the girl from the palm tree house. You could see the tree from three miles away. Vultures would fly and take refuge on the tree when they smelled a plague coming. Hasan never learned where these vultures came from. Were they even birds? When they came to the village, schoolboys and girls would stand in groups for safety. Although the vultures were a terrifying spectacle, their nature was quite calm. They did not eat the food the humans served them. Still, Morzina's grandmother would send her over with food. People in the village made fun of her, they said the vultures were her in-laws.

Morzina was very embarrassed. "I don't want to go. You go," she would tell her grandmother.

Her grandmother told her not to listen to other people. One had to show mercy to living beings, only then would Allah be pleased. After the country was liberated, the vultures were not seen as often. People said they had seen too many deaths and had too much to mourn.

When the vultures took to the air, they would run over the boys' and girls' heads, jumping like planes taking off from a runway. Hasan would watch amazed until the birds grew small and disappeared in the sky.

Morzina used to say, "Don't touch my feet, you're older than me."

Hasan would say, "I am only twenty days older than you."

"Well, older is older," she would say, "even if it is just by an hour."

Whatever it is that brings the vultures, Hasan fails to pick up the smell. Still, his insatiable soul wanders past Morzina's reading room to breathe in a little of that chlorophyll-infused air. He can still hear the ruffling of vulture wings on the palm tree. This tree, the pride of the village, would undergo immolation, a misty flame of dark smoke bringing its dignity to tatters. The fire that caught on November 24, 1971, was a different color. Hasan's house had burned in that fire—he remembers it clearly. They had to take refuge near a wetland about three miles from the village.

Hasan's family gathered under the date palm tree of their house that winter morning. The cold, yellow light fell on their raw skin. Morzina came through the mustard fields. One could see the pollen from the mustard flowers sticking to her feet. The yellow suited her fair demeanor. Perhaps she had applied it herself. Hasan remembered the wonderful lines from a poem by Jasimuddin: *The longing for the yellow through a garland of mustard / The peas come out of their veils for the kiss.* They were supposed to get juice from the date palms on their tree. Khalek tied a towel to his waist and climbed the tree like a squirrel. The thumbs in his two feet were bound together with a string of jute to help with the climbing. Khalek stared down at the cauldron hanging from his waist. Chomir shouted, "Khalek! Khalek! What are you looking at?" Khalek replied, "Snakes have left their skin in the juice." Hasan felt sad hearing it, as any child would who heard such news. Chomir, however, understood Khalek's cunning. No one would want to drink date palm juice after hearing such a thing. "Bring it down, either way," he told Khalek. Under the guise of inspecting the inside of the cauldron, Khalek inserted a straw and drank a fair amount. This was why most never called him for help, even though he was a master at climbing trees, even those others were scared of.

The village elder Fotae Bibi had foretold, *Khalek will die falling off a tree.* Whenever Khalek climbed a tree, many anxiously waited to see if the prophecy would come true. Many had become disillusioned with

Khalek for not dying yet, some even with Fotae Bibi. They would get Khalek to climb a tree to see if he would finally meet his end. Khalek didn't mind; he found it amusing. He would pretend to lose his balance to get their attention. Today was no exception. With the cauldron held tightly in his right fist, he had his other arm wrapped around the slender, rough body of the palm tree. A few steps down, his left arm slipped from the fog-wet stem. Hasan closed his eyes, unable to bear the horror of him falling. The other kids were more concerned with the loss of the palm juice than with Khalek's well-being. The adults weren't certain he would be safe, either. Chomir had his hands outstretched, hoping to catch the man. Yet Khalek regained balance within moments. He kept hanging off one end like a branch, then brought his two feet around the tree again. Chomir said, "Bastard, this is how you will die one day!" Hasan's father, Abdul Mottaleb, decreed from within the house, "From today, no one will let Abdul Khalek up a tree." Hasan had never seen his father's orders breached. No one would dare have Khalek climb a tree again. Yet Fotae Bibi's prophecy would come true one day, despite his father's prohibition.

Khalek had almost come down with the pot when Hasan's brother Abdul Gaffar and his uncle Shafiuddin hurried in with the news. "The military has arrived in the village. We couldn't stop them. Leave now." Khalek let go of the palm juice cauldron, which landed on Hasan's head and broke. No one understood this event, given the magnitude of the news they had just heard. Even Hasan couldn't understand it. The sap ran from his hair down his face. He tasted the sweetness, he started shaking, his teeth started to clatter. Chomir grabbed his hand and brought him into the house.

Waking from that reverie to the Falgun morning, Hasan has difficulty finding meaning in his work and in the bleak regularity of life.

Nevertheless, he prepares to head out. It is important for him to arrive at the office on time.

When he steps into the office, one of his coworkers Masud Alam says, "Looking for your girl, my friend? She's joined the Prime Minister's entourage."

The guys at the office often tease him about Bilu. Hasan says, "Nothing new about it, my friend. Didn't she accompany the Prime Minister to China a few days ago too? Someone has to do the job for the paper." The lack of respect his compatriots showed Bilu bothered him, although he was not that progressive either. He admitted that the presence of women in the office created excitement but also sometimes stopped him in his tracks.

The newsroom, he forgets, is a place of constant war, where the contention between its inhabitants is more intense than the actual wars they cover. Hasan is often annoyed by the other male reporters' taunts. They know something happened between Bilu and him, and they never forget to remind him. That he is a married man now does not seem to hinder their nefarious suggestions. Bilu too is aware of such shenanigans, though as far as Hasan can tell, she does not mind. She does not care, Hasan thinks. When a person cannot accept the textual and practical knowledge given to him, he is regarded as having little intelligence. When you do not provide an avenue for education for women, how can you then slight them? After all, Lilabati, Bhanumoti, and the wife of Kalidas were known to have intelligence of the highest order.

Hasan and Bilu were friends in college. Bilu has chestnut eyes, and they called her a cat because of it in college. During her freshman year, she suffered a great many of these taunts. When she answered a question in class, someone would say, "Meow." At some point, she must've accepted this fate, must've started enjoying it too. This came to be what she was known for. Hasan was amazed at her ability to withstand and survive. When they became fellow journalists, they really hit it off.

Hasan couldn't unravel the mystery of what happened between Bilu and him. There are references to such mysteries in the Holy Quran. One of Allah's ninety-nine names is *Baatin*, the one who is hidden. The blood in our veins rots to pus. It reeks of foul odor. Oh, the torment of this foul blood! What else have we kept hidden other than the stench of our blood?

If Bilu is on another international assignment, what's the harm to him? He isn't being passed over. At least, he does not see it this way. Bilu has always been the smarter of the two. He often felt she could better handle a situation, better take advantage of it.

A lot of work has piled up on his table. Hasan will have to go through it in the midst of his meandering thoughts. Four people at the office have been promoted, the second time it has happened in three months. The newsroom is now absent of any new sub-editors. There are five people in one corner; two work during the day, three at night. The role of a sub-editor is hard to establish in a newspaper. They are like the housewives in a middle-class family, holding down the entire fort without getting any credit. The Editor doesn't recognize you, no matter how proficient you are. You are entitled only to his jabs. The sub-editors in the corner shake in fear of their continued existence. It reminds Hasan of Tolstoy's *Kholstomer*. How precisely the life of a man atop an animal is drawn out—it makes one wonder if it's really a horse or an ongoing transformation.

The Supreme Court has adjourned the hearing in one case. This news from BSS must be covered by the sub-editors as well. Hasan calls themselves paraphrasers. His coworkers hate his use of it. It sounds bad, at least to the sub-editor. It "degrades" their profession. They reason that one shouldn't call a blind man blind to his face, although the truth is anyone in this city can cover these stories with ease.

The case was about Elida McDowell, an American. She brought three kilograms of heroin hidden on her body. She had an affecting face, much like the addictive qualities of her drug. She had smuggled heroin outside her skin. The British had taken away gold and brought in opium two hundred years ago. She said she did it for her boyfriend. Hasan was well aware of the penalties paid by the hapless for the cause of love. He has been covering them since he's had this job. Such people seem ever ready to take the leap for their loved ones, in spite of their significant others' refusal to do the same. Men and women had lived together and divided their labor for eons before one was given any semblance of equality akin to the others. It is to society's detriment today that women are not allowed to have their rights completely. Hasan understood this in principle, though he could not shake off the social inertia that led him to behave like a typical man.

In a different news item, France had conducted a nuclear test at Moruroa atoll. The president had said they were in favor of nuclear tests. There weren't many protests about it. People in Melbourne had held a rally. They put up posters of the president with the words, *Wanted: Environment Criminal.* Couldn't there have been a rally here in Dhaka? The opposition has called for a three-day strike here, even though the strikers do not know what the result of this strike will be. Couldn't there have been at least a half-day strike against the nuclear tests? Hasan wonders if he should call one. However, he loses his enthusiasm after discussing it with his coworkers, who treated him with ridicule. He has another idea: to hang a poster around his shoulders all day that says, *This Earth is mine*; at night he'll leave the poster at the French embassy. Perhaps the largest protest he heard about was that a company in Japan has decided to stop selling French alcohol. Greenpeace once pursued a boycott of German products to save the North Sea from environmental pollution. This seems to him mere politics, merely beer foam, only hype. The sort that profiteers like. They kiss this foam every once in a while, whenever their bait is taken. Hasan hates reading about this on a daily basis.

The Editor calls Hasan to his room. Hasan feels his chest thumping. He starts to perspire. He doesn't know how to talk in front of that man. He stumbles over his words. Most of them don't have a reason to talk to the Editor anyway. Yet the Editor calls him in sometimes. He says he is biased toward those who have merit. Hasan doesn't know if he is one of those, though. Anyone can get a good result in college like he did. The importance of these results only goes so far. At some point, friends and coworkers say, he did so well at university, yet he couldn't do anything of worth afterward. Some would go further: "He couldn't even draft a letter properly. I asked him a question about spelling. He had to check the dictionary to confirm it."

Hasan quickly combs his hair before entering the Editor's office. He does this quietly—the Editor likes obedience. If it was any other job, he would've gone beyond this. The Editor says, "If I wanted to be referred to as *sir* I could've been a minister or secretary." But when they call him *bhai,* that isn't any less of a title. Hasan doesn't understand why he had to be called in. They punish people in absentia. They wouldn't even know what they were being convicted of. Perhaps he will arrive at the office one day and see that his job is no more. He'll be handed a letter. They'll say they're going through financial difficulties. That you had given good service, that they wish you well in our future endeavors and the accounts department will take care of your dues. But they never do. Hasan has seen a lot of dramas on TV about the plight of primary school teachers and their pensions. There's been a lot written in the papers too. Journalists like him had written about it. One and a half years ago in this office, Jalal was terminated. Every day from nine to five, he would come and sit in front of the accounts department and worry about his children. But he never got his dues. Hasan knows why—Jalal never got around to being in the union.

The Editor has called in Hasan, so he could read him his poetry. Hasan's fear disappears. Hasan used to write poetry too and has published a few works in newspapers. But he doesn't write anymore. Why he used to in the first place and why he doesn't anymore, he has no idea. He doesn't even know if it's a good thing or not. A few lines of poetry appeal to him once in a while. The feeling doesn't last long; it fizzles out. Yet there was a time when he thought that life was incomplete without poetry. Now he has trouble differentiating between a complete and an incomplete life. Hasan knows he won't like the Editor's poem. The blessed direction his life was supposed to go—has it gone there? We do not audit ourselves. We write an editorial and expect others to call and praise us. If not, we praise ourselves. This is how we become a hotshot Editor one day. Hasan has no respect for such poetry, yet he readies himself to utter a few words of hollow praise.

Later that day in the office, Alam asks, "What are you up to, my fellow translator? Hurry up with your work today. My wife and I must head to a birthday party of our daughter's friend!"

Hasan is upset. "How many more birthdays must you attend? Are you going with your own wife or the colonel's?"

The others are whispering. The reporting editor sits opposite them. No one shares anything with him for fear of the entire office hearing about it. Alam is also unbearable. Once he used to write stories, some of which had been printed in newspapers and magazines. Now he only thinks of women. He has been dating a colonel's wife, who was having the affair to get back at her husband's infidelity.

Alam shows Hasan his new watch. "Made in Switzerland!" he says. "You can stay pure, like Father Sergey."

"You can celebrate your watch after work," Hasan says and returns to his work. He looks at Elida McDowell's picture for a long time. How could a stranger look so fascinating!

Alam says, "Did you know these are sahibi diseases? Before the British had arrived, we did not have gonorrhea or syphilis. There were only ailments of the stomach." He snatches the picture from Hasan's hand. "Don't fall in love with the picture, my fellow poet!"

Hasan waits outside his office. He lives about five kilometers away, and at a quarter to two in the morning, the only viable way to reach home is using the office's taxi service. Most days, he doesn't get the transportation on time. He has to wait, which is annoying. Many papers these days have bought their own cars, but their policies have hardly changed. Their drivers are aggressive on the road, thinking the journalists would save them with their powers. Yet these powers aren't like any other—they cannot be applied everywhere. It tends to reside with the police and the criminals. It depends on whether one has a better relationship with the owner or the editor. Of course, these days the owners themselves are editors of their papers. You don't exactly need to be a journalist now to be an editor.

Hasan waits an hour for the transport before heading for the bus. He wonders if he should walk home. He finds himself enveloped in the night's affections, like a shy monkey hiding its face within the trees. He doesn't come outside that much during the day. The sunlight gets to his eyes. The Lord has created the night for us to rest, but Hasan isn't privy to this gift. He has been left out of the Lord's blessing. Perhaps through his own actions it has come to this. Who can walk on like a simple man anyway? Who is able to stop in this darkling light? Slowly, he abandons all hope for the bus and walks. Dhaka at night has a different sort of beauty, like the nights one reads about in the novels of Arabia. Like the hungry heart of Meher Ali that longs for the poet's freedom, Hasan finds himself longing for something exceptional to take place. Anything other than loneliness and the anxiety of seeing a familiar face on the road.

The drivers here are the kings of the road. Their company owners have a link with the politicians. Of course, they have nothing to be annoyed about. They could simply turn the engine off and squat with their vehicle.

After walking for a while, Hasan stops near Fakirapool round-about and sits there. He is in no hurry and has no worry that a car would leave him behind. The trucks, baby taxis, and rickshaws—the giants and machines that trawl the streets during the day—have cleared out. Hasan takes a long drag from his cigarette and looks at the sky. It's a full moon. He realizes that no one in the city notices the moonlight anymore. Its intensity rivals only that of the sodium lights lining the streets. Yet, for ages, the moon has woven its infinite myster-ies and tugged us along its gravitational path. That web is torn now.

Hasan is in no rush to be home. He will unlock the door himself and enter alone. Of course, he had to do this even when Fariha was at home. She could not stay awake into the night. At first, she was afraid to be alone at home. Later, she often fell asleep with the lock turned.

To pay his last respects to the vanishing moon, Hasan joins his hands in tribute and remains seated. He goes by these streets every day, yet so much of it he fails to notice. One day this will lead him to dream about leaving home. Burned in the moonlight, standing on the plains of the moon. Streams of water bursting out of his body, drowning the moon with it. A sea creature sits at the bottom of this sea, his mouth wide open. Hasan hears the moon being absorbed inside it. He is trying with all his might not to meet the same fate. Hasan stays alive, but the moon has drowned into the unending stomach of the monster below. Inside it, Morzina, the maiden of the moon, sleeps. Countless such maidens are asleep in the land inside the creature. He has listened to stories of these maidens from his grandmother under the mysterious light of this very moon.

In the starlit sky, this moon hangs like the sagging breasts of his grandmother. He tries to clutch it in his grip. He calls it toward him, singing the rhymes of his childhood. *Come on over, Uncle Moon, leave a mark on my forehead.* How painful it is to think that the youths of tomorrow won't be adolescents anymore. What element of adolescence will they grow up with? Their lives will end turning over things at the house. There will be no moon for them, no cow's milk, no grandmother, even the absence of a companion like Morzina. All they will have are the magical boxes. The usable parts of their virtual women. The consumerist consumption of their bodies. How this business ties women down in shackles of discrimination.

On his right, he sees a woman sleeping on the island peacefully, using her right hand as a pillow. The dividers reflect off the lamp-posts and on her face. The trees on the divider are not yet the size of a human, yet their branches are drooping down to the ground. How nice it looks! Spread out like welcoming arms for the birds to find sanctuary in before they fly off into the crenulated gold soufflé of clouds. Hasan doesn't see them as trees, rather as shrubs of bonsai. They remind him of the reflections of forests in Jibanananda Das's work. Yet what else will grow in these dividers? Hasan thinks of Manik Miah Avenue, the only street in the capital that looks like an opening to the world. For a long while, it held its position as the marquee road. A road like this, in a country so poor! The hungry and dark-skinned people from the villages come to see it, huddling on its sides. Workers from the NGOs huddle by them. The sweat of the garment workers hangs deep in the air. The long lines of skeletons laid out like brickwork, building the foundation of their votes, building the Gonobhaban. They say those who beg for our pity and plead with their hands for food are the real owners of that palace.

It was the year 1001. With bare feet, a bare body, and a hairless head, Tenpa Dhonden of the *Charyapadas* had said, *I may not have my home, nor my surroundings / Nor is there rice in my pot, yet my morals are intact.* No kingdom could decree their language gone. The old Magadhi Prakrit, Gourio, and Bangla that have stayed uncompromisingly constant. But the Goddess of Time continues to devour the galaxies of our universe with each passing moment. At this time of the night, Hasan seems able to traverse through time and space, his preoccupations growing on a galactic scale.

A swarm of mosquitos drink blood from the neck of the woman lying on the island, as if it is cheap local liquor. Mosquitos are said to be quite refined in their taste. They favor healthy, good-looking, and nice-smelling bodies. They consider these attributes seriously before sinking their needles through a person's skin. Not just any human body works. But Hasan doesn't go near her, why should he? The woman, is she even real? If she was a genuine human, shouldn't she have a place to live? A home made of straw or the caves of our ancestors. The need to have a form of roof over our heads—isn't this what separates us from other animals? He finds himself drowning in the eternal dusk of this city's concrete forests. So deep the sunlight is unable to touch its surface. In this shadow-less earth, this woman slumbers like a reptile.

His elbows on his knees, Hasan abruptly notices two girls standing in front of him. They look like they cannot be more than thirteen or fourteen years of age, though they could be older but malnourished. This is often the case here. They are wearing cheap red lipstick and have used a little make-up on their cheeks too. Each girl's hair is tied in a ponytail. They are barefoot, like the beggars on the street. Their skin is brownish, with sharp eyes. Could they be sisters? They have the subtle resemblances that siblings share. Hasan looks at the two girls helplessly. Looking at them, he cannot help thinking of the women in his life. Bilu, his coworker and friend. His wife, Fariha.

"What do you need?" he asks. "Why have you come here?"

They reply in unison, "Take us. Take us with you."

Hasan extends his hands to pull them toward him and has them sit beside him. The three of them sit close together. He wants the warmth of their bodies. The warmth of brothers and sisters, fathers and daughters, husbands and wives, and between lovers. He rests his hands on their shoulders. He brings out a cigarette from his pocket.

"Won't you give us one?" the girls ask.

Hasan says, "You girls smoke?" He gives them two, along with the matches.

They light up with great dexterity. Perhaps they smoke regularly. Perhaps they too have a demon inside that they want to kill with the poison of nicotine. However, he knows that this comparison does not work. How could he compare his sorrow with their sadness?

He wants to know their names. Where is their home? Do they have a father? The older of the two can only remember a little. She says their father brought them from Baghdad to try their fortune here. They had been living in strife, dealing with plagues, droughts, and despots—no worth for their labor. Unable to feed them, the father had thought of poisoning his daughters. But killing—that is a great sin! Forbidden in their religion. So they wandered frantically from villages to towns to great citadels, the way Hagar had to seek water for her infants. Their long voyage still hasn't ended, they haven't yet reached the India of their dreams. At some point, dacoits killed their father. The daughters were sold to an emir. They have come here after a great many changes in who "owns" them, yet their eyes still have a spark, dreaming of the subcontinent, of finding their father. But they cannot return. They are stuck in this cycle. For a thousand years cursed into this never-ending cycle where they still stand.

The younger girl's memories are vague. She remembers going with her friends to the fields to play, picking out a few yams to eat, then suddenly being chased by a few vicious-looking creatures. They looked human but were white. They had planted their nets near the fields. Their bodies were mutilated by the sharp chains of their nets. They took the girls on ships and sailed them far away. Encased in darkness. They could not get out of the ancient ship. They didn't know anybody there and didn't recognize any language. All they found was that they were given food when they gave them their body's toil. Thinking of this, Hasan feels numb. Who says there is no slavery today? Can we really tell our children the truth about these heinous acts? This brutality, this greed—is there any end to the mentality of those who would loot others' bodies and futures for their own gain?

As Hasan nudges between them, the girls take him to be a willing customer. The older girl presses her small breasts against Hasan's arm. His body reacts. Hasan feels like his body must be someone else's. It has to be, or he won't be able to explain this away. He remembers he hasn't had sexual intercourse in a long time. His wife is at her parents'. She went there two months before she was due.

For this to happen under the open sky! He curses himself. What is the relationship between husband and wife? Is it based on trust or a sense of responsibility? After all, isn't everyone in a secret relationship with themselves? Before he succumbs to his thoughts and acts on them, he stands up and moves away from the girls.

But he is a poet, and he wants to be a writer. He could write a novel about the girls' sorrow and misery, the path they have taken. Perhaps they had been abandoned by their parents or sold at an old slave market. As a writer, couldn't Hasan talk about these painful situations, though could he ever feel them?

All of a sudden, a police van sweeps past from the police lines. Hasan doesn't notice it, but the girls always pay attention to such things, like deer looking out for their predators. "Sir, the police!"

Hasan grabs one girl's hand and pushes some money into it. The girl, surprised and in need, takes it. He wishes he had more to give her, but it isn't safe to carry more than that amount of money.

The police van heads for the two girls first. They flee into a narrow gully. A couple of constables jump out of the van and run after them. The girls are caught, unable to run anymore, still holding Hasan's money in their hands. The constables tear away the notes. They search each girl's body ruthlessly to see if she has more money. The two girls stare like helpless goats.

After they let go of the girls, the van moves toward Hasan, who has by then walked away from the island. The van stops in front of him. Hasan is scared of the police. Despite the things he has seen at the newspaper, he isn't used to their presence in all walks of life.

"Get in the car," two of the constables tell Hasan, adding some insults. "We'll show you for fooling around with a street whore!"

Hasan's ears are hot with anger. He has never been in a situation like this before. He feels like striking the constables on the head. How dare they slander him when he hasn't done anything! But he can't get away from them by acting like a goon. They'll run him to court in the morning, and he'll find himself in jail. By the following night, everyone will know that he was caught by the police for doing such things. Fariha won't take this lightly. He won't be able to show his face if his in-laws get wind of this. Of course it happens to others, but when someone does this sort of thing for real, they work very hard to make sure very little gets out. We all act pious until we get caught.

Hasan can see two ways out of this. He could give them some money to save himself, or he could introduce himself as a journalist. The first option is already lost to him. He has given what little money he had to the girls. He never thought this would happen when he left home that morning. Even though the money he gave the girls is now in the police's possession, he can't exactly tell them to let him go. They won't listen. Hasan knows this.

A stubbornness presses within him. He won't mention his profession, he won't take advantage of his position. Why should he operate outside of the law that binds the fate of all his people?

When they push him into a room devoid of windows, doors, and even vents, Hasan thinks he didn't do this right. The smell of urine and cigarettes is suffocating. Catching himself before he trips on another man's knee, he looks around the holding cell. It must be no more than fifteen by twenty feet. No opening to let air in, though there are huge bars out in front. If the steel collapsible gate is shut, there's no way the prisoners won't die of suffocation. He wants to light a cigarette to save himself from the smell of urine. But a search of his pockets yields nothing. The loss of his cigarettes intensifies how dejected he feels. He stares at the others locked here with him. Who can he ask for a smoke from? There is anxiety and a fear of the unknown in all their faces. They will be hauled to court in the morning. Perhaps many don't even know why they have been caught. Perhaps some are like Hasan and were merely returning from work late at night, meandering under the moonlight. The police have brought him here out of hope, per-haps—and habit. It's become quite difficult to be out on the street without paying protection money these days. Hasan can't find the courage to ask for a cigarette from the inhabitants of his cell and decides to approach the policeman on guard. He goes over to him and asks, "Police bhai, can I have a smoke?"

The cop is annoyed by how he asks this. No one talks to the police in this way. They are referred to as *sir* or even *ustad,* for they teach the prisoners the way a truck driver mentors his helper. They help them improve their skills. The officer standing guard has no cigarettes with him and asks Hasan for money to buy them. Hasan doesn't have any. Annoyed, the officer withdraws the hand he extended toward Hasan. "Your father doesn't own this place," he says, "You can't have a ciga-rette just because you asked for it."

Moments ago, Hasan still thought he was different from the oth-ers. That he has come here to observe the fun. That he is here out of journalistic curiosity. But now reality has set in. His fate is sealed with the other prisoners here. He sympathizes with them, he thinks of them as his brothers. But as time passes, he comes to terms with the fact that he hasn't committed a crime, so what relation does he have with them? How can they not understand that he is better than them? He is a journalist at a reputed newspaper. There is no point to him observing this. Their shared misery does not bring people together, it flings them apart. He wonders if it would be better just to introduce himself to the officer-in-charge and get himself out of here. But how can he get access to him? The way he was treated just for asking for a cigarette! He can't imagine how they'd react if he asks them now to bring their boss here. They have other things to do too, he figures. They make this wicked city livable.

A constable slides open the collapsible gate. His mustache was one to see! Hasan has heard that the police pay allowances for their officers to groom such mustaches. The constable's eyes are red like watermelon seeds. They look like they won't fit inside the eye sockets and may pop out at any moment. Hasan hasn't seen anyone with such oily, black hair before, as if they'd burned oily bamboo sticks for a long time to make it this black. The mustachioed policeman enters the cell to look for someone. A quiet man is seated with his head on his knees beside Hasan. His left jaw has a cut, his chin is curved to one side. His nose is flayed like a jamun fruit. His skin is dark, and he has a head full of hair. He is maybe twenty-five to thirty years of age. A deep fear is reflected in his eyes. The mustachioed policeman is going to take him for questioning by the officer-in-charge. He grabs him by the hair with his fist and yanks him up. The man tries to remain seated and holds on to the constable's legs. But the officer kicks him in the face. Fresh blood starts to pour out. Hasan is frightened of blood, he feels his body melting at the sight of it. His head starts to spin, he begins to puke his guts out.

Hasan doesn't remember anything after that. He wakes later from an agonizing dream, embarrassed. He had seen the old village. Morzina's house. The palm tree beside it. The fields where they played beyond it. A mosque to its west. The field was crowded. A meeting was taking place at the balcony of the mosque. Hasan's teacher and the head of the school, Moulavi Abdul Kader, was present. Hasan used to kiss the man's feet when he met him. He was Morzina's house tutor, he used to live in their home. He taught Arabic at the school. Hasan remembers being taught by him in Class VI. He doesn't remember any Arabic now. He only remembers that *khubjun* means bread. It was for this bread that Abdul Kader had left the village of his birth, perhaps his beloved wife and children as well, to seek sanctuary in their village. It was for this bread that he said his prayers five times a day with the villagers standing behind him. How can that bread be forgotten? Even though the arbitration today was not about the bread.

Moulavi Abdul Kader was all-powerful in the village. Whoever he would punish would have to take the punishment with their heads bowed. The chief of the village was seated beside him. Without him, Abdul Kader couldn't pronounce his fatwas. Everyone was waiting anxiously as the proceedings began. They knew the punishment that this crime called for: being stoned to death while being buried in the ground up to one's waist. Anyone who touches the guilty person's body would become impure as well. Today, of course, it would be difficult to get away with such drastic measures, what with the police and the courts, and with the passing of generations, the maulanas have discovered new, more agreeable forms of punishment. The day of judgement in Hasan's dream had stirred the quiet village into a frenzy. Even on Eid there hadn't been such a celebration. In unadulterated village life, there were few other forms of entertainment. Here, the primitive joys of fighting against the union of our bodies took precedence.

The accused, Yassin, had allegedly entered his widow aunt's house on the night of the new moon with a black cloth tied over his face. The aunt hadn't divulged this; it was Anjera's mother who saw him coming out of her house. Yassin's aunt and Anjera's mother hadn't spoken in a long time. A few years before, Anjera's mother's husband had disappeared. People in the village said he left because he could not bear his wife's anger. But the fact was that he was selling sarees from village to village. He sometimes stayed away for days and even months on business. Anjera's mother correctly understood that her husband was in love with someone far away and that one day he would leave her forever, so she started behaving like an intolerable wife, so the villagers did not blame her husband for leaving her for other women. Of course, one night or early in the morning, her unsuspecting husband might appear again. After spotting Yassin's movements, she told Peyara about the incident the next morning. Peyara's mother, she knew, was the village's unpaid mouthpiece. She could spread any news in a short time.

The neighboring villages got wind of the news that day. It was a Friday, and Abdul Kader had just about started to give his sermons when Roushan spoke up. "If this injustice isn't punished, we won't pray in this mosque from now on."

Others stood up to support him. "We have only one thing to say. If you don't resolve this, we won't pray here anymore. The times are dark. Judgement Day isn't far away."

The maulana assured Roushan that he would hear his grievances after prayers were over and make a decision. No one could pay attention to their prayers that day. Everyone was too excited about the proceedings that would take place afterward. Abdul Kader realized the importance of the situation. He said, "My devoted brothers, you have spoken correctly. It is a difficult punishment for a crime of this stature. Are you all ready to see it take place?"

The others responded in unison, "Yes, yes! We want to see strict measures taken."

The maulana said, "He will be buried up to his waist and killed by stoning. Surely, you all know the words of Hazrat Omar. He was one of Allah's favorite beings, a caliph to all Muslims. Allah said, 'If I would make anyone a prophet after my beloved, it would be him.' When his own son committed adultery, the caliph didn't let it go either. The people requested him to forgive his son, they even asked that his punishment be distributed among them. But the caliph said, 'If I do that, how will I answer Allah on Judgement Day?' He decreed that his son be rid of his impurity through stoning. Now, do we have that faith among us today? We're not Muslims, we're mice."

But the Muslims assembled did not lack faith. They wanted to see Yassin punished for his crimes. In his dream, Hasan was frightened. Would they really do this to Yassin? His head would crack open. There would be brain matter all over the ground for the cows to lick up. And where would they get the stones? There weren't many large ones in the village. Without them, how could they properly conduct the punishment according to Sharia? The stones were to pummel his soul with every touch. If he wasn't killed with these stones, his soul would never be free.

The maulana said that both parties needed to be punished, not only Yassin. But Roushan could not agree to punishing a woman in public. "All the fault is Yassin's!" everyone said, not his aunt's.

In the end, a different punishment was determined for him: a hundred lashes. Even that was carried out with leniency by the maulana. He instructed the men to bind only ten twigs together and lash his back. They would also shave Yassin's head, blacken his face, and put him on the back of a buffalo to be paraded in a circle around the village. Everyone present lauded the maulana's wisdom in coming up with these innovative measures. Their fear of the police intervening in the stoning had withered away. Yet many weren't satisfied. They thought the punishment wasn't in accordance with Sharia, merely something the maulana had come up with on his own.

That Friday, once the maulana had decreed the punishment, they placed Yassin on the back of a buffalo. Taleb Ali massaged the buffalo's horns with linseed oil before wrapping a brocade around them and placing ten paper garlands around its neck. Then, holding the reins, he walked the buffalo with Yassin around the village. A procession of people marched and danced before them. Most were children, younger than the age of ten. They didn't know what Yassin had done. All they heard was that he had entered the home of his widowed aunt. The children often went inside her house too—nobody punished them for it. The adults said he committed adultery with his aunt. But they didn't know what that meant. Electricity hadn't arrived in the village yet, nor had the magic box, through which commercials featuring Madhuri's breasts, Karishma's thighs, and Sridevi's buttocks would hasten the boys' advance into adolescence and then young manhood. The bony, uglier Karishmas around them wouldn't be able to hold the same magic anymore. But that wasn't the case yet in this village.

The leader of the band in the procession, Dhuli Mubarak, was rousing their usually drab village into a flood of festive joy. Men visited their in-laws, wives visited their parents' homes to mark the day. The rhymes the people sung that day found their way into the village's folklore. Even today, one can hear villagers singing a song like this:

Alas, what has fate brought us in this Kali Yuga
Yassin seen sleeping in his aunt's bosom
Where do we keep this shame?
The day of reckoning might come soon

Yassin had been dressed with great care. Hasan wondered if it was this absurd creativity that made them God's greatest creation? They brought Dhiren the barber to shave Yassin's head. He took one swing of the razor, then stopped, demanding a bonus, given the festive spirit, maintaining that it would be a disrespect to his occupation otherwise. The crowd began to throw coins of copper and tin at him. Dhiren shaved Yassin's head and poured a bowl of whey over him. The others took wood ash from beneath their pots and pans to darken his face.

No one could recognize Yassin when he was on the buffalo. He didn't look like the man who would buy Hasan lollipops, who still had his jolly demeanor even after failing his secondary school exams three times. Now he could do nothing but participate like a sacrificial animal on Eid. He looked like a conqueror arriving at the capital he had captured, with hundreds of soldiers and marching bands to announce his magnificent arrival. After a while, he started clapping like the others. Roushan hit him on the back.

Recalling the scene, Hasan couldn't understand why the buffalo had been so sad, with tears in its eyes. They slaughtered the animal on the school field that evening, in front of a thousand onlookers. By then most people had forgotten about Yassin. The buffalo had taken Yassin's sins upon itself and given its life for them. Everyone now became desperate for the meat. Buffalo meat was a favorite, and today's animal held special significance. For a long while, this would be a story worth telling. If they didn't get a share of this meat, they would be left out of a special occasion.

As Hasan visualizes these events at the crossroads between dream and reality, he remembers what happened afterward. Now that the villagers knew of Yassin's sin—doing such things with one's own aunt!—their knowledge would not leave him alone. So what if the maulana had tried to save him? A week later, the villagers found Yassin hanging from a tamarind tree on a clear field a short distance from the village. A desire path ran beside the tree. The sky was pink and blue, the evening's yellow spreading out from its edges. The crows bringing dusk flew away into nothingness. As an adolescent, Hasan had yearned to touch that horizon and the world beyond. Yassin had touched the horizon. His body hung vertically against the sky and the ground. Roushan, going out to the river to answer the call of nature, discovered him on the tree.

After Yassin's death, he was seen wandering from one end of the sky to the other in the blink of an eye. He spent some days roaming around the village. He visited his widowed aunt's house in a veil like a bride and cock-crowed behind her house. A day after, he prayed on the mosque balcony. Rahim Miah, on the way to the mosque to call the azaan, passed out screaming after he came face-to-face with a naked ghost. People began to describe Yassin as the village's naked pir. They said he had become a man of God, with miraculous powers vested in him. The story of Yassin, therefore, ended with attention to his nudity. Many in the village said his thing was quite big.

Yassin had dressed himself one last time before the hanging. He had dreams of being a hero. Clad in armor, returning from war, winning the villagers' rights. A tall bamboo stick in hand, with a tunic and a red gamcha on his head, he would march toward the village like

Napoleon Bonaparte. The women and the elderly would line up with candles, young and old shouting, *Victory to Yassin,* or, *Allahu Akbar!* And Yassin would pay his respects to the village elders with humility and grace. Yet before these first victories could be enacted, the defeat of Waterloo came for him. Still, the dreams in our unconscious are tied to the realities around us. Freud said that our repressed desires take the form of photography in our head. We stage these images in our sleep. The reality of Yassin's sexual desires were seen differently by him, not as something to be punished. This was why when the villagers found him hanging from the tamarind tree, he had shaved his head and blackened his face as before. His clothes were on the ground, and he was wearing only a seamless robe. Perhaps he didn't need any other clothing, for God made humans in his stead. Here Yassin's story ended.

Roushan died three days after finding Yassin's body. Before his death, he'd had a fever and kept vomiting. Everyone was unsettled by these incidents in the village. No one dared to go out of their houses, for fear of encountering Yassin's spirit wandering in the nude. As for his aunt, who was never seen in public without having her saree draped over her head, covering her face, Hasan cannot remember what happened to her after this incident. When events from his childhood bubble up and merge with everyday matters, they become disassociated from specific circumstances.

During this dream, the inner world at the crossroads of sleep and waking, of silence and language, that exists in the folds of our brain cells, nudges Hasan to merge his real-world situation with what happened to Yassin. Instead of being put on the back of a buffalo, he realizes the police have fastened a two-and-a-half kilogram brick to his genitals. He is wandering around the mosque, which turns into a police box. His genitals crumble from the weight of the brick. He can't walk straight anymore. He remembers that when he was circumcised, it took quite a while for his genitals to heal, and he had to walk slowly in his lungi. The pain he remembers wakes him up.

Hasan opens his eyes to see that he's lying on top of a high table. A ceiling fan buzzes over him. It isn't dawn yet, it seems. He remembers spending the night in the cell and vomiting. Is he in the hospital? But there is no smell of bleach. The table he is on is actually the one in the room of the officer-in-charge, positioned against the wall the way beds are lined up in doctor's rooms. Like the one the doctor asks you to lie down on as he checks your heart rate or your pulse. Hasan doesn't understand why a police station would have a doctor's bed. Do patients come here too? Or does whoever comes here *become* a patient? Perhaps the accused are laid out to be molded as the police wish. Has the same thing happened to him? Hasan feels pain in his abdomen and back. He doesn't remember a lot. He feels suspicious when the OC addresses him in a friendly manner. He has never been in a police station before, but he's heard of their remand tactics. Will they incriminate him on fabricated charges? Is all this part of their tactics?

The OC says, "Tell us, Mr. Journalist, how can we help you?"

Hasan accepts the warm tea the officer provides and finds his courage coming back. He thinks he is capable of many things. Journalists have made others divulge, have made the state capitulate— and he is one of their lot. The crime that was staged against him last night was a great injustice, possible only because of the misguided law enforcement in this country. He thinks he can end it with one stroke of his pen, even though he was in the wrong. Despite the negative views that people have of the police, at the end of the day, they are man's friend. The police can't do much to him, and since the OC knows he's a journalist, they likely won't hold him anymore. Hasan first thinks of asking them to return the money they'd snatched from the teenage girls last night. But when he opens his mouth, he finds himself telling the officer, "Yes, sir, of course you can help me. You can kick me in the ass, so I can bark my way out of jail like a stray dog!"

This was quite unlike him. Perhaps the situation from the previous night had affected him in ways he did not realize.

The OC had seemed like a polite man, but his eyes turned red. "I know how to fix men like you."

Bethlehem Road

Bilu is anxious about the Beijing trip. There is the uncertainty of travel, and who will take care of her new cat? She will be accused of caring only for the pet when she should be more concerned with settling down herself. She can imagine her newsroom coworkers' eyes, full of derision. Looks that say, *What is up with her? What kind of woman does not want a family?* Bilu is far more interested in deliberating why such circumstances exist, pressuring women to procreate instead of simply going on to have children.

Before she leaves for Beijing, she will have to call the neighbors. She must shop for cat food and leave clear instructions. She does not feel like doing this, but there is no other way. She can see their expressions, the condescending looks, the phrases that provide assurance on the surface yet betray an inquisitive *Why are you relegated to this?* A woman's age is measured, whether she likes it or not, with childbearing in mind. Yet to grow a new life inside her body is not the same as desiring closeness to another person. Bilu is a person of flesh and blood with something to say. She thinks many women today are simply renting their wombs out, while men play the role of donors.

Bilu knows her father is disappointed and does not talk about marriage anymore. Their neighbors, and hers, think she has a problem. She had been attracted to Hasan after he was admitted to university and wanted to spend some time with him. But Hasan did not respond. Like the other girls in the class, she had not liked Hassan's excessive self-awareness. She wanted to take care of herself, make something for herself.

Bilu remembers an incident that took place at her aunt's, who had a domestic worker named Aklima. She was about thirteen or fourteen years of age and looked even younger. She started to wear hand-me-down salwar kameezes that were too big for her. Until the day she gave birth, no one realized she was pregnant. The most surprising thing, which still amazes Bilu, was that Aklima resolutely said that she didn't know how a child came to be inside her, even though she was kicked out of the house for this. No one knew where she went with her newborn. Bilu was aware of the Virgin Mary and thought that, if Aklima too knew of her, perhaps she could've said that God had provided her with the child. But no one would have believed Aklima.

The child that Aklima had disappeared with, would it return to Bethlehem to cleanse humanity of its sins? Would the child say, "My countrymen, today you are like greedy dogs. Life has presented you a slab of hanging meat, and you're dying for a taste of it. Don't you see the birds? They are born without having to gather food. You call acquiring oil a crusade and, in my name, kill all my innocent children. Even after I was resurrected, you killed me in my own name. You don't have faith in Christ."

Bilu crossed into womanhood before any maternal figure warned her how it would happen. This was obvious to her when boys whom she had played with in an innocent childhood began to exhibit signs of awkwardness in her presence. Their reddened faces and stuttered words unsettled her, despite the comforting hollers of adolescent friendship. When she was only eleven and a half years of age, she felt like leeches were crawling inside her and cutting up her intestines. Blood was gushing out. She might bleed out and die.

When the women in her family had realized what was happening, her grandmother told her mother, "You cut a cake on every occasion. Cut one today in Bilu's honor. I'll pay for it."

Ma said, "You make a big fuss over everything. Why do we need a cake for this?"

"Why not? My Bilu has become a woman today. This should be cause for celebration."

"This is nothing to announce. I don't want everyone knowing about this. If people see us with cake, what madness, would we be able to show our faces?"

Bilu's grandmother was adamant. "If we can celebrate boys being circumcised, why not this?"

"If people know we celebrated this, it will be hard for me to find a suitable match for her," Ma fretted.

"Those days are long gone! This is a more significant day for Bilu than any birthday."

"You can do whatever you want," Ma snapped. "The older you get, the more childlike you are becoming!"

Bilu doesn't remember there being any cake afterward, but her respect for her grandmother deepened that day. She finds comfort in comparing menstruation with the moon's rebirth, the way the moon has to recede before becoming complete again. The female body, similarly, goes through a cycle of change to become whole. These droplets of blood and dead cells may not be of use on their own, but without them, life would not be possible.

All these thoughts conjure strange images in Bilu's head. Perhaps the males of the species are like snakes whose tunnels are wrought elsewhere—her body convulses at this thought. No, she doesn't want to think about it anymore. But it isn't easy to cut through the web of one's thoughts. We are not the masters of our bodies, we are its slaves, and we do not exist without our enslaved bodies.

Bilu makes a mental list of the things she must do before leaving for Beijing. She has only had the cat for a few days and hasn't settled on a name yet. People will find it strange that she cares so much for it yet has not humanized it. She does not feel the need to anthropomorphize it. She is disgusted at seeing cats and dogs being given human clothes to wear. She understands that cats and dogs have been humanity's companions for millennia. Even in our faith, where dogs are seen as dirty and to be avoided, dogs have been granted the high honor of being mentioned in the holy book: a dog had accompanied a band of people fleeing religious persecution and guarded them for hundreds of years. Moreover, in the *Mahabharata*, when Yudhishthira and the rest of the Pandavas were on their final journey to their resting place, a dog befriended and accompanied them until the end. When Draupadi and four of Yudhishthira's brothers died along the way and Yudhishthira was left alone with the dog, Indra had arrived with his chariot, welcoming Yudhishthira to ride on it. Yet knowing that the dog would not be welcome to accompany him, Yudhishthira refused. The dog had become his companion, and he would not abandon it. Eventually, the dog was welcomed.

Bilu goes to her bedroom to retrieve her cigarettes. She needs the temporary solace they offer. It is a habit, not an addiction. She can go many days without it, though it is also impossible to quit outright.

Does God really claim two lives for having sex outside of marriage? Bilu wonders. Is any ambiguity possible in their interpretation? She bites her tongue at the thought. The mullahs would be discombobulated at a woman attempting a tafsir. Has anyone ever heard of women interpreting religious texts? Yet the first convert was a woman, and the Prophet was aided by women throughout his life, with Khadiza and Ayesha playing important roles. Indeed, who cared for women more than the Prophet?

Bilu considers an example in the Old Testament. When two angels visited the prophet Lot as two handsome men, his neighbors accused them of having bad intentions. Lot then replied, *Take my beautiful daughters, but do not insult my guests.* The Scythians of Sodom weren't satisfied with that. For this reason, God could not tolerate the inhabitants of Sodom and Gomorrah. However, the pleasures of homosexual ejaculation were nothing new. Perhaps it has been with humanity since the dawn of creation. Why else would early writers place so much importance on it? Apparently the Greeks took more pride in being with men than with women. They only got married in order to have children. Plato's description of love isn't any different for women or for men. Of course, one would be forgiven for thinking otherwise after hearing the story of Helen. Bilu has read of similar descriptions about love between men in the *Baburnama*. It was not uncommon even in colonial Calcutta. After all, one sometimes even sees a buffalo mounting another. However, society seems to ignore outright the love between two women. Bilu doesn't remembering hearing of a punishment for this.

Bilu has been in the shower for too long. The trembling cold can only be assuaged by the warmth of another cigarette. She's twenty-seven and six months old—is she still an eligible, marriageable woman?

There's a saying that Bengali girls are considered to be old ladies at twenty. But Bilu's body doesn't look it. She has beauty, more or less, or at least grace. She read in one of D. H. Lawrence's works that there was no difference between the two, that the body will express sensuality as long as one possesses it. It's what attracts the opposite sex. Bilu doesn't have a shortage of that. She knows it by the way her friends and colleagues take in her body. She has spent her entire life dealing with the vitality of her womanhood.

Although girls these days don't graduate until they are twenty-four, then enter the workforce, the girls that Bilu studied with in her village are now preparing to get their daughters married. When the monthly bleeding that annoys Bilu stops one day, it will take with it her ability to create life. Men too are subject to their genetic codes. Even if a man stays young mentally, he will still grow old physically.

Bilu remembers when she was assigned to cover the anniversary of the birth of Rabindranath Tagore. The academics put the bearded man on a pedestal. Even today Rabindranath is still the refuge of the middle class, someone easy to have faith in. Bilu wonders what he would make of her thoughts. She has immense confidence in the poet. His songs bring her peace and are a tonic for her exhaustion. The wonderfully strange sensation of voice and words on the human body are like an enchantment, the way snakes dance to the tune of snake charmers. Though, nowadays researchers claim that snakes cannot hear, that they merely move their bodies to the flute's movement.

At the age of seventeen, Rabindranath traveled to Britain to pursue a career in law like his brother. He had enjoyed his stay with a few families there, even if he hadn't enjoyed academia. As someone who was motherless, he had the pleasure of staying with a Scottish doctor and his family of three daughters. In his autobiographies, he had mentioned them by name. Perhaps such arrogance wasn't taken well by the young poet's father, who called him back home. At his departure, the doctor's wife had cried, holding his hand. "If you had to leave so soon, why did you come at all?" she asked. When Rabindranath returned to Britain ten years later, he had asked about their whereabouts but couldn't find them, which distressed the young poet immeasurably. Bilu sometimes wonders: No one has written more than Rabindranath. Perhaps no one will in the future as well. Even so, was he able to write about all that tormented him?

What if Bilu had been married at his wife's age? She would be surrounded by grandchildren now. His wife's name was Bhabatarini, but the poet wasn't satisfied with it and renamed her Mrinalini, which means a multitude of lotuses. According to tradition, there were four types of women, the most qualified being the Padmini—a woman of superior intellect and beauty. Bilu doesn't know which category she falls into, though she can't be a Padmini. If she were, she would have already been in a blissfully happy marriage. As a child, Rabindranath had played kanamachi with his Marathi tutor Annapurna Turkhud. Her father, the doctor Atmaram Pandurag, later went to Calcutta to appease his daughter's longing for the poet. But they couldn't get the poet to return her affections. The history books do not mention her as the first object of his love. Before her, there was perhaps Kadambari Devi. It has been said that one of Rabindranath's ancestors was made an outcast from society for accepting food, out of desperation to survive, from a Muslim. Bilu has recently learned that the word *Tagore*, which is an Anglicization of *Thakur*, has an Islamic origin: it originates from *Tigir*. The word blended into Bangla during Turkish rule. Even though it is said that Brahmins don't nitpick on race and caste that much, the Tagore family proves it wrong. Rabindranath's marriage, after all, followed Hindu tradition. The family had to settle for Bhabatarini, the daughter of an insignificant employee, in order to match their caste. The poet had to marry within the contours of his estate, no in-laws' house to speak of.

Bhabatarini became a mother at the age of thirteen. If this happened today, the poet would have been arrested on charges of statutory rape. The *Prothom Alo* daily has published many statistics about the rape and torture of women. A court in India recently ruled that parents will be held accountable for rape if they marry off their underage daughters. Rabindranath had married off his daughters at a young age as well. Of course, he can't be solely held responsible for this. The expectations of marriage, childhood, and sexuality are controlled as much by society as by individuals. People have fought dearly against this, seeking to remove laws that hurt individuals at the benefit of society. In the nineteenth century, many took the risk of protesting against polygamy, child marriage, and sati, the act of burning widows in the funeral pyres of their dead husbands. But perhaps the poet did not think much about this. Even if he had, it hasn't been reflected in his life. Vidyasagar and Ram Mohan did and are recognized as social reformers, whereas Rabindranath is a poet. Reflecting on Rabindranath, Bilu considers that he not only laid down roses in the path of liberation for the future but also strewed some thorns in their path.

Bilu doesn't feel like going to the office today. She's been on assignment for many days, and whatever she had to report on, she's sent it off. She has nothing new to write about. She has had a talk with the Editor regarding this on multiple occasions. She understands these assignments mean nothing. What is really important are the Editor's blessings. One cannot survive easily without them, no matter how many university degrees one holds. Moreover, one cannot ignore the importance of a woman's looks when it comes to the prospects for her career and marriage. Bilu has no trouble accepting this. She also understands she won't have any worth left if she hands her body to anybody. One must learn to strategize. Everyone has to learn how to survive on their own. A wrong turn can prove disastrous. Men can be lecherous toward women. Women too, but a woman always has to prioritize her safety.

Bilu thinks about the recent murder of a journalist couple. Bilu felt cold in her body when she heard the news. She lives with only a cat to accompany her and her landlady. As a precaution, she has added a collapsible gate, keeping it locked most of the time. But fear does not come from outside. It is within.

She remembers how she landed this job. There wasn't much competition, but she had used some tactics nevertheless. She had joined the newspaper as an intern in her last year of college. The organization had been reputed for two things often lacking in journalist openings: a guaranteed job and a regular salary. In other professions, these two are seen as conditional to a good workplace. But Bilu knows journalism hasn't yet become a profession. Even though wage boards are declared regularly where the salary structure isn't bad, most owners do not pay their staff on time, let alone pay them according to the wage board, especially as all the industrialists each want to have their own paper. Journalism is a profession where no one can tell one's true intentions. On the face of it, it's treated as work that's independent, but at every step, it's stained by dependency because the journalists do not own their paper and the owner has a big say in how the paper is run. Many journalists have sacrificed their lives for the truth. Many owners are in favor of pursuing the truth as well. If newspapers are not allowed to be themselves, how can a nation develop? Bilu has heard that the government is in the process of instituting new policies to regulate newspapers. Journalists have objected to this, but it would do no good for journalists are now divided into two camps, one of which is dedicated to fulfilling the wishes of the government at all times. Divide and rule—wasn't this the British policy? The British have left, but their ghosts remain. Journalists are now either ruling party journalists or opposition party journalists. It's as profitable as politics, this business.

On her way to work, Bilu realizes she has forgotten to check on the cat. She considers herself intimately attached to the poor thing yet is quite forgetful toward it. She will deliberate on that later when she reaches home. Now she must hurry. The Editor has urgently called her in for a meeting today. She has a bad feeling but cannot pinpoint what it is exactly.

Even when pushed to the brink of death, doesn't a snake hold on to its companion? What does that female snake have, a priceless thing that no one is aware of? The eggs that women hide in their wombs— the ones they received from their grandmothers. The chain of this womb reaches back to the one who birthed us all. On a whim, it had divided, and the Almighty had to create a male counterpart to hold on to life, to forever chase women, to go back into that womb. All of men's pleasures are hidden in women. Women, too, have their pleasures in men's hold. In each other's company, the desire to reproduce is ignited. Sometimes this takes the form of a war. Everyone must play the game. It becomes dangerous to deviate from it.

It's Friday, a dull day. Usually there isn't much news. The government offices and courts are closed. Journalists don't gather outside secretariat buildings for quotes and news. Usually they prepare a few exclusive news stories beforehand about the plays, lectures, and poetry recitals that will dominate the weekend. People like a bit of leisure after a week of work. But this news doesn't satisfy their readers and lulls them to sleep. That's why the Editor writes his commentary on Friday. His words are highly valued. The readers eagerly wait for his editorials. Of course, the Editor needs to make substantial arrangements in order to write. He likes writing while feeling quite relaxed. That he considers this activity a celebration wouldn't have been apparent without seeing him. He writes the whole thing by dictating it to someone in the office. One person will take it down for a few days, then someone else will take over. Everyone understands by now that he doesn't have a particular favorite. He likes keeping everyone busy. Within a few days, he exhausts himself. That the man is unhappy is obvious. Why else does a man drink in his office? Even his drinking he does like the characters in Bengali films, openly from an expensive tumbler. Monir the peon will take care of the details. He'll bring ice from the refrigerator and keep it in a clear glass bowl. The ice cubes will be arranged on top of one another. There will be tongs for the ice. Beside it, a porcelain bowl full of cashew and pistachio nuts. It isn't a grand arrangement, but it looks clean and precise. The Editor never offers alcohol to whomever comes in to take dictation. He himself rarely sips at it. But he smokes continuously, using the dying flames of one cigarette to light the next. The only exception has been with Bilu. She has told him that she can't endure cigarette smoke. That she feels like throwing up or has a headache from it. That her father has had to quit smoking for these reasons, too. The Editor often jokes that the tobacco companies will be out on the streets if it was up to her.

Perhaps the most absurd thing the Editor has told her is that he is not addicted to smoking. That he really is just a social smoker. He does not inhale the tobacco smoke, he lets it out. One can't do journalism without smoking. Without it, it becomes harder to find common cause to relate to others. He thinks one cannot be a writer without drinking and smoking.

On the days Bilu is made to take dictation, she takes sips of Coca-Cola from her glass in between listening to the Editor and taking notes. Today, his topic is social degradation and cruelty. The past week, a mother had murdered her two school-going children, then committed suicide. This was after a scuffle with her husband, who had been having affairs with other women. No one thought it would lead to such tragic consequences. The city's inhabitants were in shock. Who could really be blamed for these deaths? The husband's attraction to other women was nothing new. Bilu wonders how far human cruelty can go. She wants to ask the Editor whether we are continuously heading for entropy. Where will our civilization end up?

However, as she raises the question, she suddenly does not feel well. She starts to perspire, the room feels smaller. Bilu can't understand it. She has a headache. She is slurring her words, they do not sound like her. She has had the soda and cashews before—it didn't have this effect on her. Was there something in the Coke?

The Editor asks, "Bilu, are you okay?"

He gets up and places a hand on her shoulder. She rests her head against the rails. The Editor tries to drag her to the sofa. Is this what he wants? She loses consciousness.

This might not be the first time something like this has happened to her. In university, she had celebrated the New Year with her friends at her dorm, Rokeya Hall. The hall's general secretary, Shabnur Apa, a senior, was there. Though he was a couple of years older than her, he liked her a lot. Bilu didn't understand the concept of celebrating on December 31st. Why did one have to spend the day drunk, why couldn't the day be memorable without the drinking? Now she knows she was thinking like those small-town people. Mofussil mentality, one that doesn't fit in with the city's festivities. The New Year celebrations that happen in the cities do not resemble those in the villages. Being separated from the people close to them has led to an intense desire to recreate and reimagine their ancestors' rituals. Today, of course, Bilu thinks celebrating the end of the year without drinking is tantamount to celebrating a birthday without a cake or celebrating Bengali New Year without panta illish, the traditional soaked rice and fried hilsa fish. Perhaps years ago, the Bengalis had celebrated the day similarly with homemade alcohol. The indigenous people still do it. What people think of as their own creativity is really their ability to imitate. Their descendants inherit their habits and see what they were able to imitate as truth.

Bilu has been in poor health for a few days. She suffers a lot of mental and physical stress during menstruation. Perhaps her passing out has something to do with her childhood fits, which she had before she began menstruating. Only her close relatives knew about it. She would be studying in the morning while her mother was busy in the kitchen and her grandmother was keeping an eye on her younger brother Shafik. At first she'd start to feel drowsy, then she would discover herself under the palm tree. The tree would jettison up from the earth into space, taking her with it. It would soon take the form of a huge bird, its bushy head transformed into the imaginary seabirds of heaven, the ones she heard about in childhood. She recalls the story of the creature who abducted a princess to protect himself from his fate and kept her hidden on a desolate mountain. She was guarded day and night, but one day a prince showed up to reclaim her and they were married. Though at first the creature was in despair, he later realized that one couldn't cheat fate. For Bilu, these surreal moments occurred in the juncture between sleep and awakening, truth emerging through abiogenesis. In earlier times, when there weren't stark divisions between humans and animals, one could procreate with the other. The epics of Homer, Valmiki, or Vyasa are full of such stories. How Zeus rapes Leda in the form of a swan and she gives birth to Helen. How Sita was born of a plowed field. How Draupadi remained the pinnacle of femininity with her five husbands. In those days, sages would ejaculate whenever their desires arose, and from those emissions would arise impossibly powerful people. Dreams are a species' history of their memory. Human children laugh and cry in their sleep because of the anguish of being separated from their mothers in the hunter-gatherer days. How else could Bilu make sense of waking up from a dream of a swan lusting for a snake? Of course, Bilu couldn't recollect all of the dreams later. She could only feel a reptile slithering up her anally and twisting her intestines. She had woken up in that torment, in a panic from her fits. Her throat would turn sore from the crying and moaning. She would call for her mother, but no sound would come out of her. Her family was in a constant state of fear regarding her illness. Medical attention didn't come to any conclusion, either. Her family had to resort to fakirs who specialized in Jinns.

Fakir Manikchad decreed, even before seeing Bilu, that it wouldn't be possible to save her, for the very prince of the Jinns had set his eyes on her. Even though she hadn't turned nine yet, she was a compatible age for the Jinn. Jinns didn't take into account one's size, weight, or age. They could pass through the eye of a needle. The prince of the Jinns had seen her when she was strolling by the river with her hair down beside her grandmother. He jerked his chariot to a halt; sixteen winged horses flew out. Bilu had seen this scene often, painted on the back of rickshaws. The creatures were neither female nor horse but an amalgamation of the two. Perhaps within those portrayals lay dormant the anxiousness of men to mount them, their dream to be the master. To get on top and ride away up to the skies.

Fakir Manikchad had taken Bilu's grandmother and her mother aside. It was the crown prince of the Jinns who had fallen for their girl. The old king had grown frail. He might diminish any day or abdicate in favor of his youthful prince. It was imperative, then, for the prince to find a suitable mate. The fakir wanted them to wait for their destiny to change, to not throw the opportunity away. Bilu's grandmother felt proud of her granddaughter. Not everybody had her luck. The Chowdhurys in their area had gotten rich in this way. Asmot Chowdhury had sold off his land to send his son, Hashem, to study in Calcutta. A Jinn princess was studying there too. The wealth of these Chowdhurys might have decreased after the British took over, but their beauty had never known any bounds. It didn't take long for the Jinn princess to fall for the boy. The king couldn't deny the longings of his only daughter, although the princess had to convert to Islam to marry him. They were married in the Kingdom of the Jinns. Afterward, the Chowdhurys became rich overnight and bought all the land nearby. There were stories about Hashem's younger brother traveling on the Calcutta train and pulling the emergency brake again and again. When the conductor came by to see what was going on, his servant would pull out a stash of notes from his shoe and hand the man a fifty taka note to pay the penalty for the misdemeanor. Bilu's grandmother had seen the Jinn princess with her own eyes. When she was Bilu's age, the princess had visited her in-laws' estate quite a few times. Everyone was in awe of her. They would look at her expectantly, as if she could take them to the Jinns' country at her mercy. She was tall, fair, and had a pretty face. Bilu's grandmother hadn't seen a more beautiful woman in all her years. After Bilu was born, she thought she was the princess, reborn in her own son's house. After she saw the symptoms of Bilu's illness and heard what the fakir had to say, she realized there was no need to fear. The prince of the Jinns would one day arrive and take her away to be married.

Educated, modern people who do not believe in tales of marriage involving Jinn princes should acquaint themselves with the story of Dushyanta and Shakuntala. If they have difficulty understanding Kalidasa's Sanskrit, they can turn to Vidyasagar's Bengali translation. King Dushyanta was chasing a male deer on a hunting trip only to get lost in the forest. He came upon Shakuntala at an ashram, and his heart began to ache for her. There were laws in his kingdom to deal with such circumstances. The king's power was supreme, his words were law. That's how it had been for five thousand years. If the king was attracted to a young, unwed girl, she would immediately be brought to him. In the days of King Dushyanta, one called this marriage a Gandharva marriage—one based on attraction. The king made the beautiful Shakuntala his own with a ring and completed their act of union. He assured her that she could come to his court whenever she pleased, but if she wanted to claim the title as his queen, she had to bring the ring he gave her as a totem. The king had many wives—how would he know as well whether the claim was true? While the king might be able to forget this excursion, as many such events occur during royal hunting trips, the orphaned girl living in the ashram in the middle of the forest would never forget the king. She had nothing to give other than her labor. She was always accompanied by the other girls in the ashram under the watchful eyes of the sages. They were the first to notice the physical changes in her. The king might have pursued lovemaking merely as an activity of pleasure, but it nevertheless led to the creation of life.

Bilu's grandmother had dreamed of traveling to the land of the Jinns at an old age through her granddaughter. However, Bilu's mother did not take the news lightly. Her only daughter, falling prey to the Jinns—how would she live without her? Even though Bilu's grandmother wanted to cut a compromise with the Jinns, her mother didn't agree. She told Fakir Manikchad, "Please tell us how we can protect our daughter. We'll pay any amount necessary." It wouldn't be easy chasing away a powerful Jinn like him, the fakir had said. But he assured them that, if not alone, he would get the help of his Lord. Everyone knew his powers. He kept evil Jinns imprisoned in bottles, and everyone could hear the Jinns' screams when they were punished at night. But before calling on his Lord, the fakir wanted to try it himself. For this, he needed a raw pot on which he would sit and call out to the old Jinn who was about eighteen hundred years old. He rarely summons such elderly Jinns, for afterward he loses much of his energy and can't get up from bed for days.

Bilu's cousin Salam was entrusted with bringing the pot. Salam had thought nothing of the job. What was so difficult about it? They could be found nearby in Palpara. The Pals' son Sudhir was in the same class as he was. They were good friends too. Even though Sudhir was a Hindu, Sudhir liked Salam's company more. Salam would often visit their neighborhood and watch the artisans at work. The myriad ways the earth can be molded on the rotations of the pottery wheel—Salam has trouble believing it to this day! But when he told Sudhir what he needed for the fakir, Sudhir stared at him for a long while. "No, Salam, it isn't possible for a son of Pal to do this. You may take any of the ones that are already made, but we can't give it to you raw.

This would go against our profession." Salam was surprised and hurt by this. He didn't understand why this was so. How could his friend refuse him? Was it because he was Hindu? Perhaps they all really were the same, whether Brahmin or Shudra. They'd do anything for their superstitions. Salam didn't recognize that what he had asked of Sudhir was based on superstition too.

Sudhir said, "For every Pal, this job is like their own child. These are their own creations. The earth used to create them has life. No one likes to destroy an undeveloped life. Your sister Bilu is like my sister too. Why wouldn't I try to help you? But I can't. As a Pal, we gain knowledge through this earth. We fulfill the needs of men with it the same way the Lord made humans from the earth."

However, Salam was able to steal a raw pot. But he hadn't needed to. Bilu's father strongly objected to any form of folk beliefs and saved Bilu from the fakir's treatment. He had consulted a doctor friend, who assured him that her condition was due to weak nerves and would go away with the aid of vitamins and by following some guidelines. Nevertheless, Bilu's friends remained curious about her situation. Her friends would ask her how the Jinn's thing felt. Bilu didn't know what they meant by "thing." Though she was in the same class, she was shorter and younger than them. Moreover, she was quite absent-minded due to her frequent illnesses. By the time she began to understand these things, her father had been transferred to a different posting, and she was at a different school. Later an old friend had said, "You've become so beautiful because there was the touch of Jinns on you." She now understands that humans experience all their knowledge through their sensory organs. Perhaps we can't explain the invisible, immortal world of our consciousness. The greatest claim of consciousness is that it does not perish, especially in the case for surviving after death based on one's good deeds. Forever it cries, *I was here once, I still have a claim to it.*

Later, Bilu couldn't remember anything after passing out in the Editor's office. She had woken up disoriented. Perhaps she was dreaming it all; perhaps it was real. A morning a long time ago. Their living room was crowded with people. Some sort of arbitration was going on. Women were whispering in the halls. Bilu was young, but she was aware of the differences between men and women. She had learned that women shouldn't go out in the presence of men. That men do things to women when they find them alone. They try to insert their thing inside them. And when their own weapon isn't strong enough, they wouldn't mind inserting a pistol, bayonet, or a knife.

Back then, no one called it rape in their village. They referred to it as *zina*, a word that does not encapsulate the intensity that *rape* does. Broadly it meant an illegitimate relationship, without the implication of assault. A rude boy in her class had asked their religion teacher what zina was. The hujur said, "It's when your father goes to see a street girl instead of your mother." Bilu had asked her grandmother what rape meant. She said, "Men have a venom-sac like snakes; when it fills up, they must empty it out. They grow crazy like snakes, whose blood heats up at the sight of any person. Men are like that. When they encounter a woman walking by, they want to sink their fangs in. Remember never to waltz around random men. Men you know do it too. Always remember to wear a veil when you go out, so that men can't see you." Even though Bilu doesn't follow her grandmother's advice, she remembers it every time she gets dressed to go out. Her grandmother had said, "Women die from rape the way people die from snake venom." When they don't die, they still sport the symptoms. They can never stand straight. Molina couldn't.

She had been missing for many days—lost, disappeared. Her family wasn't really distressed; she had gone missing like this before and returned too. After a couple of days of silence, crying, and meandering here and there, she would go to her aging father, Lokman Sheikh, and caress him and cry, and be part of his father's family again. When Molina was seven or eight years of age, her mother had died. Cholera was rampant. There were floods too. People could not find a place to bury their dead. They would perform the last rites on boats and dump the bodies in the sea. The hilsa fish had grown quite fat eating the carcasses. Those who had eaten those fish were the ones who got cholera that year. There was no hope of surviving after contracting it. They would vomit until they had emptied themselves out. They were not allowed to touch water, as people thought adding water to their system would only exacerbate the situation. Thus they would experience dehydration, which would result in blood clots, and then die within hours. Nowadays, even a child knows how to save themselves: drinking water with a pinch of salt and a handful of molasses reduces the chance of dying. This knowledge that children now find so simple was a matter of grave complexity for the sages back then.

The year Molina's mother died of cholera, her two-year-old brother had drowned too. Her older sister Ambia had gone to her in-laws' village after her marriage. She returned after hearing of her mother's death. Lokman Sheikh's financial situation wasn't good. He used to take cloth from the village to sell in the towns. It would be months before he returned and gave his wife some money. At night, therefore, when he was away, other men would try to visit his wife, but before her marriage, Ambia would keep a billhook out front and they wouldn't come near. After his wife died, on the advice of the village elders, Lokman Sheikh remarried for the sake of Molina. But the new wife didn't stay for long.

A girl without a mother was a tempting target for predatory men. They would give her lozenges in secret and try to get her into their laps with mangoes or tamarind. When Lokman went away for his business, he would leave Molina with her grandmother. There, the affections she received were in the natural order. When she was older, she would go over to Bilu's house and help her mother with the chores. Bilu's mother was affectionate toward her. Wherever Molina was during the day, she would return at night to sleep at her grandmother's.

The last time Molina had returned after going missing, rumors circulated in the village that she was pregnant, even though she wasn't married yet. The talk was that she had been sleeping with men. Even when Molina explained what had happened to her, no one believed her. She said that when she was returning to her grandmother's place, the Special Forces camped at Paramanik's place had picked her up. For about twenty days, they held her in secret. At night, ten or twelve of the men would rape her. All her crying and pleading didn't work. Apparently they had told her, "You're a slut. This is what you do. What's the problem? You'll make good money." Molina had trouble recognizing who could be trusted and who couldn't after her mother passed away. She didn't understand the relationships between men and women. She couldn't keep anything secret, couldn't refuse anyone anything, either. Everyone in the village had seen street dogs trying to mount their female counterparts on the streets. Cows, goats, chickens, and ducks—the same custom worked in all their cases. But it was different for human beings. Molina did not know that. The absence of a mother prevented her from learning so. Molina only knew, through the horrors of her experience, that sex was something men found pleasure in and that, even when women didn't want it, they would be forced into it.

When news reached the camp that the Chief of the Special Forces would be making an inspection visit, Molina was released. The soldiers had warned her, "Slut, if anybody hears that you were here, we will kill you." Molina returned home and told her grandmother everything. Her grandmother wanted to know if the soldiers had done anything else to her. She knew the kinds of torture the Pakistani military would commit on girls, inhuman violence to other parts of the girls' bodies.

Molina's troubles were not over. Returning from the ghats after bathing, Kabil's mother noticed Molina was walking like a pregnant woman. She knew her expert eyes couldn't be wrong. She asked right away, "Slut, who knocked you up?" Within a day everyone in the whole village knew of it. How it had happened wasn't important to them. Molina didn't specify a name, and anyway the man who had done the deed wasn't going to be found. For cases like this, there needed to be four credible witnesses to the event. Anyone found to have testified falsely would be gravely punished. Not a single person could be found to testify that Molina had been a victim of rape. However, Molina's unborn child would be the strong proof against her—the child whose face had yet to feel the sun and the wind. If she wasn't punished, despite the evidence present, everyone around mother and child would be accused of being complicit in the sin.

Even though the proper time to conduct the arbitration would have been after Friday prayers, the people of the village chose to do it at home on the morning of the holy day, out of consideration for the girl. They met at Bilu's uncle's house. The elders sat on top of a charpai over the living-room grounds facing an open courtyard of about two thousand square feet. Women neighbors were watching from the edge of their curtains. Most people stood in an arc around the courtyard. Young boys were forbidden to attend. Malitha's eldest son was given the responsibility to see that this was so. He had a crook used for cows to deter any boys trying to peek in. Lokman and Molina sat on the grounds, leaning toward the village arbitrators. They weren't looking at anybody, not even at the people present. One wouldn't have guessed that the day's arbitration concerned their behavior. Molina's saree, once a bright red, had turned drab from days of wear. It wasn't long enough to cover her entire body. She sat with it bunched up, one end pulled over her head like a veil.

It was Malitha who spoke first. "Listen, Lokman, we can't all be victims of your daughter's sins. She has gone missing before. She goes out at all hours of the night and does not obey our judgement. The incident this time is worse. If we do not punish this, curses will rain down on us!"

Someone from the audience spoke up, "Shave the bitch's head, pour whey over her, and kick her out of the village!"

This kicked off a furor among the people gathered. Malitha raised his voice, and they calmed down. He asked the imam seated beside him, "Hujur, what is the punishment for this crime?"

The imam looked frightened, as if he was forced to be here. Slowly and vaguely, he said, "There's no discrimination between man and woman in Sharia. But there's a prohibition on punishing pregnant women. The unborn child in the womb has not committed any wrong. Until the child is born and has had its mother's milk, the girl cannot be punished."

The way the imam spoke, many thought he was against disciplining her. Perhaps the way the fatwas of mullahs are written these days, they had to be cautious about such things. The police involve themselves in these matters. Or perhaps the Alia madrasahs have changed their views. Anyway, those present weren't content with the imam's words. Everyone wanted to see the girl punished immediately—in front of them. They expected the usual: shaving her head, blackening her face, throwing her out the village, or exiling her. Even lashing her or a combination of punishments, as had happened in Yassin's case. They were disappointed with the imam. Regardless of what Sharia says, everyone was in the favor of immediate retribution. One couldn't do everything according to Sharia all the time. Whatever punishment was meted out, the village's greatest fear was having a bastard child born in the village. All the neighboring villages would come to know about it. Their reputation would be in tatters. No one would want to marry their sons and daughters to the families in their village.

Malitha came up with a solution. "Both father and daughter have to repent. Molina's hair will be cut from the ends, the way women have their hair cut before going on a pilgrimage. Molina will be lashed with ten twigs bound together ten times. This will be equal to a hundred lashes against an unmarried girl's back. Lokman and his family will have to isolate themselves from the village for forty days."

Everyone approved of this judgement. One or two of the people said, "What will become of her unborn child? We can't let a bastard child live here. Throw her out of our village."

Unconscious in the Editor's office, these scattered memories float inside Bilu's head. One fails to understand the material world while passed out. Without thinking, one cannot live. She must talk to her neighbors later. The pet has to be taken care of. She wonders if, when she gets home, it will still look at her in the same way. Will she be the same Bilu? Will this passing out change her position in the newspaper?

Is the Beijing trip still happening? Everything Bilu has seen and experienced in her life is staged in her mind. Molina's unborn child did not free her from her body. Bilu thinks that Aklima was luckier with her pilfered impregnation than Molina. The absence of her parents saved her from being punished. Moreover, her pregnancy was advanced before it caught anyone's notice. Even though Bilu does not know where she is now—has her child survived, or is Aklima still wandering the roads of Bethlehem? Bilu wonders: Why did Christ wander the streets amid the vagabonds, lepers, fishermen, prostitutes, and the marginalized? He used to listen to them and preach to them the Lord's word. He would say: Those who do not have fathers have the Lord himself as their father. They were the children of God. Their fathers are among these innumerable vagabonds.

Molina's story did not end as tragically as Yassin's. After the village's judgement, everyone had gone quietly back to their homes. Even though it was late, they cooked rice with lentils and had a late lunch. When night fell, no one came to ask after them. Maybe a few days later, the village realized Molina and her father had left their home. It was winter, so there wasn't enough water in the ponds and the river to drown themselves. And since they weren't seen hanging on a palm or tamarind tree nearby, they must have left for a faraway village or town. Perhaps they had gone to a textile mill or garment factory in the capital. Their departure was good news for Malitha and the others who fancied themselves protectors of society. They didn't have to resort to going up to Molina's house and forcing them to the noose themselves, for the village could not, would not take responsibility for a fatherless child. Lokman and Molina weren't wrong in predicting that. That was why they wanted to free their child on the roads of Bethlehem.

Nazareth Road

Hasan spends forty days in prison. The officer-in-charge had tried to help him; if Hasan had kept his cool, the matter could've been resolved. The officer wanted it too. But Hasan's anger and curiosity brought them to this unwanted situation. Yet amid the lurid consequences of his actions, Hasan is comforted by Rabindranath's words. One mustn't part with the jewels of life, no matter how they rust in the dust. He longs to be a writer, that's why he reflects on Rabindranath in everything. But had Rabindranath ever been to prison? In Rabindranath's time, spending time in jail was a common experience, one of honor for the people of the subcontinent. The youth, desperate to free their countries, flocked into British jails like locusts. From within the prison walls, the young poets sang, "We feign being shackled and deceived to have you shackled and crippled." To those anxious for freedom, the whole of India felt like a prison under British rule. The Faraizi Muslims saw India as Dar al-Harb, a non-Islamic land, whose rulers might be called to the path of God. Rabindranath's efforts against British rule weren't negligible. But

Hasan had been surprised when he learned that Rabindranath didn't have any sedition charges filed against him.

Nevertheless, the reasons why Hasan is in jail are not honorable. The accusations made against him are: suspicious movement, robbery, hooliganism, and misconduct. Perhaps if he had engaged a lawyer, they could not have pinned all this on him. However, Hasan did not want one. He thought, *Let's see what happens.* A discontent was brewing in him regarding his work and his household. If he had been born in British India, surely he would have been a revolutionary, fighting for change in society. He would've thrown a bomb at Kingsford's carriage and killed the magistrate, not the two women who had died instead as intoned in the song of Khudiram. In that song, it is said that he would return, ten months and ten days later, born of a different mother to continue the revolution by any means. Whenever Hasan heard the song in his childhood, he wondered whether he was that child. During the liberation war, it was played all the time in their house. When his eldest brother went to fight in the war, the song would perturb his mother. But she didn't feel good either if she didn't listen to it. Despite their reluctance, his sister would play it multiple times a day; she understood what it meant for their mother. She would ignore all work and come over to the veranda to listen to the song and wait for news of their brother. Hasan would lean his head on his mother's chest and move with the rise and fall of her emotions. No youth today has the opportunity to achieve the glory that his brother did. The nation is now free. The motherland does not want the blood of her sons anymore.

While in prison, Hasan loses all hope in his job. The mere waiting for one's salary every passing month. The singing of praises of the government. The jumping at the throats of the opposition the moment they speak. As if all unproductivity and disorder belonged to the opposition party. No meaningful journalism happened in this government-assisted newsroom, he concludes. Even the ruling party's people considered the paper to favor them. Their own party's publications didn't support them like this. Most of Hasan's colleagues perhaps do not realize this. Perhaps he does because his surroundings don't make him think like he did before.

Even though he doesn't want anyone to know of his detention, within twenty-four hours, everyone in the office is aware of it. The crime reporter, Momin, hears about a police van taking someone away. The list of those detained by the station includes Hasan's name. But Momin doesn't at first guess it was him as no profession was listed. Moreover, it was unthinkable that someone like Hasan would be arrested. But when Hasan is nowhere to be seen for two days, some of his coworkers look into his whereabouts. A peon is sent to his house, who reports that the neighbors said he hasn't been there the last couple of days. His place was locked, and his pregnant wife was at her parents'. His colleagues can't find a way to reach his parents. Only Bilu knows the address, but she is in Beijing. In the end, Momin confirms at the station that it really was Hasan whom the police had arrested and that he had been sentenced to one month's detention without trial.

Momin couldn't believe at first that Hasan would do such a thing. The officer-in-charge said they caught him red-handed. "He started doing it on an island beside the main road around two in the morning. With not one, but two underage girls. They were women of the night, and this was just business for them. But still, there is a place for that sort of thing! One can't just do it right under the sky if one wishes. That's worse than animals. If we don't punish these people, how can the nation prosper? Don't you people say that the police don't do their duty? But when your interests are harmed, you make sure we are done for. Even so, let me say this: I did not know the gentleman was a colleague of yours. He didn't introduce himself. That's to be expected. Who can show their face after doing such a thing? He also punched a constable on the nose when we were pulling him into the van. Tell me, how were we at fault?"

No one at the office could accept that Hasan had met such a downfall. How could this be, a conscientious person like him doing *it* on an island! However, why did he go on foot instead of taking the office auto-rickshaw? Surely he had bad intentions. A man at home alone, his wife away, blood flowing to his head . . . Regardless, Momin was annoyed that the police had run him through the courts the next morning. Hasan was a journalist, he had been a student with brilliant results. It wasn't that Momin liked him. The boy was a bit snobbish. So what if he had been a star student in college, he didn't get more money for doing his job as a journalist. Nevertheless, Momin told the officer-in-charge, "It's hard understanding you people. You don't give anyone a chance when you catch them, not even your own fathers. There's a saying: when the tiger attacks you, there's only one wound; when the police do it, there are seven. You make it all work from the back, but from the front, one can't even thread a needle in peace without getting in trouble." Momin went on in jest, "You know, our mother nation is getting fucked over day and night. Hasan probably just wanted to give them a little something for their labors." He knew the police wouldn't apprehend him for saying that.

In the end, no matter how much Momin tried to keep the news under wraps, everybody knew why Hasan had been in jail. Many of his colleagues commented, "If you had to go to jail, commit murder at least. Why do something so shameless that dacoits and pickpockets are known for?"

In the later part of his detention, Hasan wonders what Fariha, his in-laws, and his coworkers will think about this. He couldn't go around announcing the reason why the police were holding him. Why *did* he give money to the girls at the island? In practical terms, perhaps there was hardly any difference between the police's accusations and Hasan's rationale, such as it was.

When Hasan is released at last, no one comes to receive him at the gate to the jail. If he were a political leader, he would have been inundated with garlands. Convoys of trucks and cars would have accompanied him around the capital, his welcome parties setting vehicles on fire, bombing cars and buildings, even carrying out murder in broad daylight or raids on the treasury—these actions would have been typical. Political leaders are greeted as if a spell in detention erases all their sins, making them as innocent as newborns starting a new life. For those thrown in prison, it's an opportunity to have their images plastered on the bottom corner of their leaders' posters, posters calling for the unconditional release and withdrawal of the apparently false accusations against the tried-and-tested soldier, a zealous warrior of the resistance against authoritarianism! Of course posters give their prime real estate in tribute to the dynastical roots of the leaders, and a junior leader has to make concessions to his neighborhood's seniors. Still, they rise in the ranks after stints in jail.

This isn't the case for Hasan. His loneliness reminds him of Yassin. A rally had been organized for him. He had been mounted on the back of a buffalo and led around the village, a hundred people surrounding him, celebrating with drums and music. Yassin may have committed a sin, but he was a cause for celebration. A leader's work is similar. He will rouse the public, no matter how temporarily.

Entering his house after forty days, Hasan feels uneasy. He wonders if he really is at home. Or has he been resurrected forty days after his death—how many days did Jesus take to return? Or is he here to attend his own Chaliswan? The number forty is quite important in religion. It is said that hellfire begins to punish the dead after they have been laid to rest in their graves and the last of the living have moved forty steps away from them. Why else was Hasan punished for forty days?

Could Hasan's punishment be differentiated from Yassin's and Molina's? His was made through the laws of the nation, the others through long-held beliefs of society. In the latter instances, the authorities were more powerful than the offenders, and there was no shortage of witnesses. In Yassin's case, the victims were absent. Those who had testified against the offender had vested interest in asking the imam and the village headman for justice. Hasan does not understand his crime and who he had harmed. The officer-in-charge had played the role of Roushan, accusing him of crimes as Yassin had been. It could be that no crime was committed in the first place, and the question of who committed the crime isn't that important. Perhaps it should be up to the nation-state to ensure that offenders are punished, no matter who had committed it. Justice has existed since the beginning of life, in the forests and the seas. It is how society tries to preserve its origins. Those who make the laws and who have the power to reform the law are the ones with the power to retaliate against offenders. This system is predicated on our sense of morality; without it, the weak cannot be protected, and the strong cannot be restrained.

In the Middle Ages, it was customary in Europe for the punishment to be equivalent to the crime. An eye for an eye, a hand for a hand, not a strand of hair more. Shylock's demand was for a pound of flesh, but that couldn't be accomplished without shedding more blood, which would call for yet more punishment equal to the crime committed. If one tribe has murdered a member of another, then a person of his own tribe must be killed to even it out. However, punishment against the king and royalty was different, horrifying, overt. The king was God's representative of the realm. There was no difference between prosecuting a king and prosecuting one's God. Only those who could claim the Lord's power could punish the king and take away his divine rights. The deposed king would lose his powers and stand trial for misusing the Lord's powers.

In Hasan's case, he was alleged to have touched the rope that bound the law itself. He had been accused of manhandling the policemen. The police were the state: they held the power to beat you to death, to throw you in a water tank with bricks tied to your body. But if you put your hands on them, that's taking the law in your hands. Did Hasan really punch the policemen when they were pulling him into the van? Perhaps he did do it; perhaps he should have done it. Anyway, he's been punished for it. Hasan now thinks that those who are sentenced for false accusations grow to believe that they really had done those things.

His time away from the house makes it hard to believe that people live here. All the objects have become active in the absence of humans. In favorable environments, in the presence of water and air, life is aggressive and continues its own lineage. Hasan lies on his back with his eyes closed for a time. When he opens them, a huge lizard on the ceiling is craning its neck to look at him. It looks at Hasan as if he is a strange thing. Perhaps it is wondering how a lizard of Hasan's size has come to be here. If Hasan were smaller in size, perhaps it would've already lapped him up with his tongue. The lizard's belly is quite large. Maybe it is pregnant and full of eggs.

Hasan wonders if he himself has turned into a big lizard, like Gregor Samsa in Kafka's *Metamorphosis*, who had woken up one day to realize he had been turned into a bug. Samsa's eyes fell on his brown, dome-shaped belly and innumerable veins curved like bows. He lay hanging sloppily, his numerous legs, slim compared to his body, flailing around horribly. Hasan thinks: Many a time, the lives we live are no better than a bug's. Even this lizard knows a lot of tricks to save its life, while Hasan doesn't. When its enemies chase it, the lizard could detach its tail and toss it at them, then hide while the enemy is distracted by the tail. Even the way the lizard catches its prey is formidable. It lashes out with its curved tongue like a whip and rolls it back just as quickly with the prey ensnared. What Hasan likes most about the lizard, something he had failed to notice before his time in jail, is its dexterity in walking on any surface, be it the floor or the ceiling.

When Hasan enters the kitchen, he jerks back in shock. Hundreds of cockroaches are running around, alerted by his footsteps. The floor is covered with rat shit, like black rice. He can hear their squeaking, it sounds like they have multiplied in his absence. It is hard to breathe with the reeking stench. Before he had left for the office the last time, the domestic worker had cooked rice for him on the stove. This was part of Hasan's daily routine. He doesn't eat out like his colleagues. He would come home, bring out curries from the fridge and heat them up; sometimes he would fry an egg too. The rice left on the stove had dried and hardened. Cockroaches had laid eggs in it and hatched their young. There are similarities after all between cockroaches and humans. That's why in schools we dissect cockroaches in the lab. The cockroach has to be sacrificed so that we can better understand the mechanisms of biology. These insects are better than us in developing adaptations. Even when other living beings perish from the deadly effects of hydrogen missiles, cockroaches survive.

The last time Hasan had left this house for the office, he had seen a couple of crows nesting in a coconut tree beside his veranda. Today, he could hear the cries of their young. Perhaps they need something to eat. Their mother will return in a few moments, he thinks. Maybe the father is nearby as well. Crows are quite loyal to their companions. The males and females share equal responsibility in caring for the young.

Hasan's appetite disappears as soon as he sees the state of the kitchen. Eating anything from there will mean instant diarrhea. There is nothing even worth using. Seedlings, large and lively, have sprouted from the onions and garlic. The absence of earth has forced them to feed off each other. Of course, this too will end when all the food is depleted.

Hasan decides to get something on the way to the office. Returning to his bed, he realizes he hasn't had sex in a long time. He pictures his wife's face. He will be a father soon. His stay in jail has distorted his sense of expectation. He recalls the date the gynecologist had given them—only about three weeks are left. However, Fariha's water could break at any time, and the child come out through his or her own strength.

When Hasan arrives at the newspaper office, the Editor tells him, "Have a rest for a few days. You've been through a storm. Let me tell you something, the world isn't how you consider it to be. Instead of molding the world to your liking, try to shape yourself to its fashion."

He also asks about Fariha. Such a nice girl! he says. He had seen her only once, at their wedding. The Editor attends the weddings of almost all his younger colleagues. However, he does not eat anything there except tea and coffee, as most of these events take place in the evening and he prefers to spend evenings in his own way. Nights are very important to him. He likes to sober himself up for later when he will raise a glass of rum or gin to his lips.

Hasan does not reply, simply shaking his head. He doesn't want to be here, he came only because he was called in by his immediate superior. One couldn't deny that the Editor was really fond of him. He indulged him like a father, as if he saw the shadow of his youthful self in Hasan. With Hasan's arrest, however, he has been disappointed. He thought this kid would make it big one day. He had brilliant exam results, he was the creative kind. He figured a young man like him needed some leeway. But a boy who fails to escape from the police when he works for one of the big newspapers in the country, who ends up misbehaving in public, isn't someone the Editor can expect much of.

The Editor says, "When I joined the profession, the police used to fear us like death. They used to respect us too. There was corruption, of course, but not like it is now. They want to eat up everything now. I mean, even if you have to eat from a tree, at least keep the tree alive, right?"

He waits for Hasan's agreement, then says, "Well, did you truly . . . no, forget it. This is your personal matter."

He starts again. "In my time, there were many brothels in Dhaka. There were journalists who went there, especially those who were assigned nearby. I went too, a couple of times. But only for the experience. I used to think I'd be a writer. That writers and journalists have to experience all sorts of things. No one talked about this, even in

Muslim Pakistan. Everyone took it naturally. Brothels play a role in protecting religion, you know? Otherwise the nation would be swept up in rape and misconduct. Those who are religious apparently have marriage contracts with certain prostitutes. The fear of the afterlife consumes us all, except for our hunger and our cock—sorry about that, I don't usually say these words. Well, you are not a child. Now there's a brothel in every affluent area, frequented by goons, police, journalists, you name it. The person who cannot marry because of a lack of money, where else would he go? The guy whose wife has gone through menopause and does not like being around him anymore, how else would he make his marriage work for the children? You might say then that women must have brothels of their own with male prostitutes. You could be right, one can't sidestep that. If physical relations aren't one of man's primary desires, why would the holy texts promise us beautiful women after our death?

"The girls in the brothels make someone sit in their husband's seat before they start work. These men eat their share of the profits by selling the bodies of the girls and beating them, while the girls give them a husband's rights. You must know the lawlessness in these microcommunities, it's part of what goes in larger society. At the same time, the law doesn't come down on these people. There is a double standard here."

When Hasan remains silent, the Editor says, "Leave it. You seem to be in a bad mood. Don't take anything so seriously. Life is there to be observed and to be enjoyed. Don't let others take advantage of you. Go, have a rest. Apply for a week's leave. As long as I'm here, you won't have any trouble. I wish you good luck."

It is not possible for Hasan to grasp what the Editor is saying. Each culture explains its nature in a different way. Because hunger is hidden in the instincts of every person; for the preservation of his being, for sustenance, for satisfaction, he is nothing but its servant. As for the relationship between man and woman, it is a normal instinct but not an inevitable occurrence. Today these relationships can no longer be reconciled with the traditions of the Old Testament. The institution called marriage is becoming endangered. When the burden of sex is reduced, it will be easier to establish equality and friendship between the two.

Hasan does not understand the significance of the Editor's words. He only wonders: why did he raise these conversations today? Did he want to tell me something? What was the catch? Did he believe the police, that I had really done those things? When the Editor had been talking about brothels, Hasan had begun to fume. He had been steadily losing all respect for the man before his run-in with the police. Now he had little left for him, although given his position, it was pointless to get angry at his words.

Since Hasan arrived at the office, his greatest concern was what Bilu would think. If it was possible for anyone not to believe that he had slept with the girls in the street, it had to be her. Their relationship hadn't advanced to a physical one in the time they had known each other, despite her intense attraction toward him, her beauty on all fronts, and her need to understand him and love him, until a somber depression had changed her view of things. It wasn't like her principles didn't play a role either; even though she didn't put much sanctity in the idea of keeping the body pure, she believed that preparation was needed before a union of two bodies.

Hasan comes across Bilu in the corridor when he is walking down the stairs. He is unprepared. She looks effortlessly attractive; what she is wearing fits her perfectly. Hasan doesn't want to see Bilu and hadn't expected her to be at the office at this time. She only shows up in the morning when there are meetings. Otherwise, her routine is to come late in the evening and leave a little before 10 p.m.

It is impossible for Hasan to avoid Bilu now that they are face-to-face.

Bilu says, "Why are you avoiding me? Are you ashamed? Oh, these are the signs of a great man."

Hasan asks, "What are the qualities of a great man? Please tell me."

"Have you ever seen someone follow one of the purest people in the world? That's because there is no debate about women's issues with them! Don't you see, the founders of all religions are quite liberal toward women. Some of them are addicted to many women, some have renounced their wives and sons and accepted sannyas, some never remarried as they were afraid of women. Hindu, Muslim, Buddhist, Christian—all are the same when it comes to this. You have a wife at home, a girlfriend at the office, now the road is not safe for you. It is not too late for you to become a sannyas, Hasan."

Hasan finds Bilu's teasing uncomfortable, even annoying, especially at this time when his mind is distracted. When he needs sympathy from his friends, here they are to draw blood instead. However, he understands Bilu's words deeply. What did Sri Krishna do to get Radha, then while abandoning Radha, he sought his liberation in the arms of hundreds of women? Gautama, the son of King Suddhodana, abandoned his wife and infant son when he left home forever. Throughout his life, he saw women as an obstacle to his holy pursuits, just as Jesus, the son of the Christian God, saw them. His own religion, Hasan reflects, has no shortage of such stories.

Hasan thinks it would've been better if Bilu had slapped him across the face. She could hit him with her shoe or stop talking to him. Clearly, she believes the accusations by the police. What does this mean for their relationship? Assuming her love for him hasn't mellowed, does her intense reaction mean that she is hurting badly?

He says, "You look quite different today. It makes me want to wander around with you the whole day."

"At least you noticed! I must be having a lucky day. I have a few things to say to you. Do you have time now?"

He jerks his head no. It would be perilous to take a walk with Bilu. He does not want the prolonged exposure. He dreads the journey home too. Tomorrow he is supposed to go to his in-laws and see Fariha for the first time since she moved back to their house. He has no idea how she will react to all this. She did not communicate with him while he was in detention, so he concluded that she did not take the matter lightly—at least, not as lightly as Bilu seems to have taken it. In moments like this, Hasan yearns to take up the life of a wandering hermit. He realizes this would be a cop-out instead of facing his present difficulties. Hadn't many men done that, left their wife and children to face God? How many of them had done it just to get away from their family? The American author Philip Roth once joked that writers in communist-led Eastern Europe relished the thought of exile because it meant that they'd finally be away from their wives. Perhaps Hasan would join this long line of men succumbing to the pressure of family and quitting the lives they had known.

He shouldn't. His wife needed him. He would rather be with Bilu, as he had thought about from time to time before and after marrying Fariha, but one couldn't just wish away one's responsibilities, as much as Hasan wanted to.

Bilu walks with Hasan out of the office, even though he said he wouldn't have time for her today. "Where are you headed? I'll accompany you for a while. I don't have much work today. You don't seem to have any, either. I know how 'busy' you are."

"Rickshaw!" Hasan calls as they reach the engineering institute and walk toward Shahbagh. There is still time before the sun sets, even though there isn't much contrast between sunrise and sunset in the capital. It had rained that afternoon. Puddles abound on the footpath, though there are no clouds now and the sky is clear. There may even be rainbows, but it's not possible to see them with skyscrapers obstructing the view. To see the whole sky, one has to lie on one's back on the green fields of the gardens of Surahwardy and Ramna and look up. Hasan had done so many times.

Bilu buys a few kinds of pickles and stands in front of a taxi. "You have no idea about women's appetites," she says. "You don't give birth, your body doesn't allow anyone inside it or let anyone take a bite out of them. Even women forget this these days. There is chemistry involved in the bodies of men and women. If women are in need of acid, men need salt."

"Is today a Friday?" Hasan asks.

"You've lost your mind. Today's a Tuesday."

"With so many people in the streets, I figured it must be a holiday."

"Weekends do not matter. There's a crowd seven days a week, twenty-four hours a day. I've been thinking that I should get married and go off to a small, mofussil town. I'll have a small farm with ducks and chickens, luffa and all sorts of gourds. I won't have to buy anything except salt. It'll be like in those bartering days. If I need to, I'll get a spinning wheel like Gandhi and weave my own sari. There will be a medicinal herb garden in the front. The goats will be milked right in front of the neem trees. Did you know proteins from goat's milk are easier to digest than those from cows?"

"This is all romanticized. You talk as if it will be luxurious work. Have you ever had to husk rice? If you had such desires, why did you break off your marriage with Ruhul? The sort of dreams you're having, he would have been the perfect man for that."

"Leave it, I've saved myself from all that."

"What's going on with you? Have you been feeling helpless about the city like me? Well, you can marry some lazy son of a landlord back in the village. He'll fulfill your wish for a dozen kids. You'd live long too, I hope."

"Do you know how old I am? You can't be any older than me. I wonder if it's too late already. I should've started thinking about this years ago. In a few more years, there won't be any candidates left for me. I have done injustice to my body too. I know you have a wife. But even as I'm aging, I still want to spend my time bantering with you, even though I know how impossible this is."

"I don't quite understand you, Bilu. If you wanted me this much, why didn't you say so before my marriage?"

"I thought I didn't want to marry a classmate then. I still loved you after that. Let me tell you, girls used to be considered old by the time they hit twenty. We'll only be able to keep this interest going until we hit fifty. When puberty is history and menopause begins, who really wants to carry along with a body like this? Where will love run away to then?"

"This happens to men too."

"Their desires and ability stay for quite some time, I've heard. But I won't stay in a loveless relationship."

"But you want to marry me."

"You know why I can tell you these things? You are my friend; it feels like I'm telling it to myself. I'm opening myself up and sharing all my filthy crimes and limitations with you. Even though you never thought of me as a friend, only as a desperate woman always hanging on to you. It's better to not claim someone who is so . . . unsuitable."

They are in front of P. G. Hospital. They will take different buses and go their own ways. Hasan will have to go to his in-laws' tomorrow, though he is hesitant.

Bilu says, "Before you leave, let's go to Silvia's for tea."

When they were in university, there weren't many good restaurants in the area. Now there are quite a few coffee shops and bookstores, yet their longing for the old and the familiar hasn't lessened. They go up the wooden stairs and sit at a single table on the second floor. It feels like the tables and chairs have been preserved in place. On the floor below, beside the footpath, kebabs are being deep-fried. They use broiler chickens nowadays. Almost every hotel now has this sort of fried kebabs and other masala-esque food ready. The food acts both as the restaurant's advertisement and object of attraction. While half the stomach is filled by the smell of the food, the rest can only be filled through consumption. Once the body starts feeling hunger, it must be fulfilled. When one leaves the table only eating half a meal, it is worse than eating nothing.

The customers on the second floor usually come in pairs and talk between themselves. It is dark inside, though the sun shines radiantly outside.

Hasan says, "Actually, you know what? The relationship between men and women isn't that serious. It's a joke made by the Lord. He has given what each one wants to the other. Look, what use would a girl have for firm breasts and a drooping navel, or men with their extra tail? The mystery of it brings about life on Earth. You remember, in the village when the animals mate, no one showed any curiosity except for a young girl. No one would question it."

"Now it's usually economically disadvantaged women who become victims," Bilu says. "The rapist usually comes from a powerful section of the society. It's only if the rapist isn't powerful and shielded from consequences that there is certainty of judgment. If it continues like this for other crimes as well, it will be as if all of society is being taken advantage of."

Bilu still trembles when she thinks of that day in the Editor's room. She still does not understand exactly what had happened—how did she lose consciousness? In her unconscious state, did the Editor behave immorally? She only remembers this much: she felt sleepy while taking dictation from the Editor, and then nothing else.

After she awoke in the Editor's room, she saw the man had a look of deep concern in his eyes. She said, "Sorry, sir, I think I fell asleep!"

Her words seemed to remove all fear and burden from his shoulders. "You don't look like you're in good health. Maybe you need some rest," the Editor had said.

But as the days went by, Bilu grew more and more suspicious. What had really happened, was something mixed into the drink that day? After which the Editor had fulfilled his dirty wish. She had wanted to ask him several times: How long was she unconscious in his room? Why hadn't he informed their colleagues or taken her to the doctor?

The more Bilu thought about this, the more she entered a dark world of fear, uncertain apprehension, and humiliation. For a long time, she wanted to share it with her close friends, perhaps even with Hasan, but she could not.

There are many accidents in life, sorrows, humiliations, defeat, the pain of losing a loved one, yet the struggle of a person's life does not stop, they have to go on—as long as the air of this world enters her lungs, as long as the blood flows into the network of her arteries, Bilu vows not to let any obstacles and insults stop her path, even if she is temporarily crushed.

At Silvia's, Bilu says to Hasan, "There was a madman in our village. I thought of him when I saw you today. His problems began with him wanting to go to jail. He also wrote a few poems, I remember. He used to say that, when the world is a prison, the government's prison is the best place to live, for one would have no worries about food. But though he wanted to go to jail, he had not done anything wrong. He tried to give the police reason to arrest him, but his efforts failed while his desire grew stronger. In the end, he made himself a cage, placed it on the balcony of his house, and sat locked in it. The people in the house used to give him food. His brothers used to say that he did this for fear of having to work. But they were also happy in their hearts, because if the brother was mad, he would not have to receive his share of their father's property."

Back at home that evening, Hasan lies down on his bed. He sees the light escape his bedroom before drifting off to sleep.

Hasan looks out the window to see Morzina. This makes him feel better. Where has she come from after so many years? She says, "Wait, I'm coming." Moments ago, his father had gone to the prayer room. Winter hasn't left yet. Fog covers the entire plain; it's impossible to see anybody within a hand's reach. He turns to see if his mother is beside him; perhaps she got up to freshen up and start the day's work. Hasan leaves the comfort of the bed. His feet pressed against the cold floor, he walks out and holds onto Morzina's hand. Then, through the dew-soaked wheat fields, they run hand in hand. Their feet are blood-ied by the sharp bundles of wheat, but they do not worry about it. Through fields of chickpeas and rye they go, up to the banks of a river, its slopes populated with the homes of bank mynas. Usually birds' nests are made of straw and up in trees, but these birds are different. They dig holes in the ground to lay their eggs. They use straw to give the eggs the necessary warmth. If miscreants set fire to a nest, the eggs cannot fly away. All the mother bird's troubles go up in smoke. The eggs Morzina's mother had inherited from her own mother to have her child have been lost to history. An indefinite fire blows all their dreams away in a coil of smoke.

A few days before she disappeared, Morzina had not been behav-ing like herself. She secluded herself like a frightened child, as if a crime had isolated her from her peers. She avoided Hasan as well. A void now stood at the back of the house where Hasan and Morzina used to discover each other's bodies under the mango groves. An infes-tation of rats and beetles was taking over the house. Mother said, "We need to kill them with Endrin." There was no shortage of powerful pesticides in the village. Every house had a bottle of it. To reduce the severity of the poison, it would be mixed with water before being used in the eggplant fields. Farmers now don't have to worry about plant diseases after the advent of the BT eggplant, which is genetically mod-ified to have resistance against pests. The environmentalists had made a fuss about how eggplant that isn't suitable for pests may not be suit-able for the human body either. There is no end to our whims; like children, our tantrums keep coming. We find fault with pesticides. We also find fault when there aren't any.

Hasan does not like recalling this story about Morzina. He had seen many girls in his village commit suicide by taking this poison, especially those who couldn't accept the men their parents had chosen for their husbands. Girls whose parents did not value their daughters' emotions. Girls whose husbands beat them for no reason or could not provide their in-laws with the dowry they asked for. Through the poison, they escaped from their humiliation. But why would Morzina mention the poison? Coming from her family, she didn't need to think about this.

What had really happened to Morzina? Hasan has wondered about this over the years. Why else would he be reminded suddenly of the Moulavi Abdul Kader tutoring Morzina alone? How did the paraffin lamp get knocked over by Morzina's feet? How did the fire take to their tin shed ceiling before burning her pajamas and kameez? How did Abdul Kader come out unscathed while Morzina had third-degree burns? Why was it that Abdul Kader had to go out at that moment to answer nature's call? No one raised these questions at the time. They regarded the fire as one of the ordinary occurrences in the village. People are lost every day from the edges of villages and towns, taken into white vehicles by white-clothed aliens from other planets, whom family members mistake for law enforcement officers, thinking that their loved ones would respectfully be returned after due questioning. But when the family goes to the police for information, they feign to not know anything; only a general diary entry is filed. The family still does not trust their words. Then their loved ones' bodies are found by the roadside, or a housewife discovers the bloated bodies washing up on the shore of the river in the morning. It doesn't take long for the family to know who had done it; it must be the special forces. But they forget that there are supernatural beings such as the Jinns. They who used to lure people out of their homes and make them slip into wet mud and sink. People were careful not to cross the paths of these abducting Jinns, even by mistake. The Jinns have now changed their strategies.

Why would Morzina want to take her own life? There had been no talk of marriage. Morzina's grandmother had said, you two would make quite the couple. His father had wanted her to become a doctor, she had good brains. Even though Hasan hadn't known of any female doctors at that time. Without a doctor, one could still get treatment, though the medication did not have any names or labels. Now doctors rule over patients like mystics and quacks hypnotizing their customers. Morzina didn't get to be a doctor. She wasn't taken to a doctor either. They laid her burnt body down on banana leaves in her mother's room. They broke an egg and applied the egg whites and yolk over her skin to numb the pain of the burning. None of the men were allowed to see her, not even Hasan. He learned that her face remained unharmed. Apparently, no one had seen Morzina cry or groan even in such torment. She tried to move her dry lips with her tongue. Perhaps there simply wasn't any water left in her body to come out. She wasn't given any water after the burning. Occasionally a wet cloth was pressed against her body. The water would prolong the healing of the wounds, the villagers had said. Though the wounds didn't need to heal. Within four days, her suffering ended. On the last day, she had trouble breathing and began to experience fits. Many said that Morzina could have survived, but her trachea was too badly burned.

Of course, Allah does what is best. Perhaps her guardians had desired her death. For if this girl went on to live, she would have had disfigured, wrinkled skin. No man would marry her. The beauty that once sparked jealousy among the people of the village would be a thing of the past. Still, her mother couldn't accept it. She begged Allah to spare Morzina's life. She vowed that she would fast and send her boys every year on pilgrimage, but that didn't change Allah's mind. Things would fall into disarray if every whim of mortal beings is taken into consideration. The fire, finally, did its job. If its power to burn was taken away, no life on Earth would be possible. Even Moulavi Abdul Kader wouldn't have been spared had he not gone outside. Allah is far more concerned with keeping his creation in order than with the glory of his name.

However, the killing of Moulavi Abdul Kader—that was unexpected. It happened before anyone could figure out what was going on. Abdul Kader was said to have come from Sudharam in the Noakhali district. The village boys would sing, *We have come seeing him shirtless with a hat / Hailing from Sudharam, Noakhali, this man.* He was light-set. One couldn't guess his age by looking at him. His goatee was a bush of black and grey hair. He was quite a pious man. Everyone liked him. He regularly served as the imam at the Zohr prayers at school. He wasn't ill-tempered like religious studies teachers usually were. When he preached in his dialect, many of those listening enjoyed it. Children would roll on the floor laughing. His topic was sexual relations between men and women. Especially concerning the destruction of Sodom and Gomorrah. How the men there were more attracted to men than women. When Allah had sent two of his angels in the guise of attractive youth to inspect the situation, the city's people lunged at them to meet their desires. The people in this region were aware of all these stories. There was another story: In the days leading to the day of the apocalypse, there would come a time when women would outnumber men. Men would climb up trees and hide for fear of women. They would ejaculate from the trees, and the women would drink the semen to become pregnant. In those days, ape-like creatures would stand guard on either side of the street with long sticks and spears and attack whoever tries to pass by. The children of the village listened to these stories, unaware of the obscenities implicit in them.

Abdul Kader would return home after the final exams every year and stay for a month before returning. He might have said he had a wife and children and an aging mother back home. But Hasan was suspicious of the man. He never acquiesced to going anywhere alone with him, for he had heard from his uncle that there were many teachers who were demons—*rakshasas*—who took human form to teach in school. They lured away the children with temptations of wanderlust. Those children never returned. The rakshasas' tongues licked them numb. Later, they were doused in burning oil in a big cauldron. Fried for consumption. Only one or two children succeeded in escaping; this was how others got to know of these things. Nowadays, these incidents happen quite often. People aren't safe because their belief systems have changed. When girls are on their way to school with their books in hand, many of their classmates or teachers offer them chocolate to accompany them. Only when it's too late do the girls realize these people aren't the ones they grew up with. That they were devious Jinns or demons who have taken the forms of their friends. Those who have lured them away grow fangs like vampires, their bloodied tongues wagging out. When their parents or neighbors see the tooth-marks on their backs and the wounds on their genitalia, they squeeze all the blood out of their body and throw them out like emptied husks of sugarcane. Their empty body is taken to the hospital morgue, where the doctor notes that the victim had been sexually assaulted before the murder. But the police never find attackers. Those influential sons are really bastards of Jinns. Why else do the police find it so hard to catch them? These bastards can stay hidden inside the state's structure. Jinns are built of fire; that's why the people of Earth cannot see them. But their character has changed. Before, Jinns would tempt women out to the bushes or the jute fields to drink their blood without killing them. If the neighbors came across the attack, the Jinns turned invisible and wreaked havoc on their house. A sorcerer or fakir would have to be summoned, for the Jinns wouldn't leave until the fakir used burnt dried pepper or sponge sandals to force them to. And if the Jinn was quite the rascal, as when they made women pregnant, there had to be different arrangements to chase it off. The sorcerers would need solitude; the afflicted would watch at a distance from behind the curtains of black cloth. The sorcerer would add all sorts of herbs to his water, then glaze it with the white cream coming out of his genitalia. The mixture would be made in front of the possessed, and the Jinn would flee at the thought of having to drink that. The presence of these Jinns wasn't anything new. There is mention of them in the Holy Quran. The Jinns had tried to seduce the Prophet himself. The verses in Al-Nas and Al-Falaq speak to such circumstances.

That's why when Abdul Kader went home every year, none of the boys thought of accompanying him. When he returned to the village, he stayed at Morzina's family's house. They partitioned their outer living quarters for him. There was no furniture except a bed and a wooden almirah. He might have kept his papers and his belongings in a tin box under the bed. In the rest of the space, he helped the children with their schoolwork. The house was separate from the main house. A rain tree in front provided shade at all times. When the fruit ripened in the spring, there was a rattle in the air. Even though Abdul Kader had come from a different district, he had become part of the village. When he returned from his holidays, people in the village would eagerly greet him. It was through him that the village's understanding had expanded to unknown places, whose mysteries swept Hasan's imaginary landscapes to Earth. It's why everyone was bewildered by the murder.

Everyone was busy preparing for Morzina's burial. Her burned body was supposed to be covered by five pieces of the white shroud. But ten portions wouldn't be enough either. Abdul Kader had advised wrapping her body with banana leaves first. He said the green leaves and green trees perpetually chant the Lord's name, so one must bury the dead with stems of green trees, ideally from date trees. The date palm tree is Allah's special blessing. It grows in the holy land. The prophets had preached eating dates.

Everyone appreciated Abdul Kader's knowledge about these matters. He knew more about their religion than the mosque's imam. That's why the imam always tried to find fault with him, although when they met face-to-face, he would greet Abdul Kader with religious salutations.

One by one the villagers scattered three handfuls of dirt over Morzina's grave, chanting loudly, *Minha khalaqnakum wafeeha nuaeedukum waminha nukhrijukum taratan okhra. From the earth we have been created, so we shall return, and from within it we will be resurrected.* In the midst of these holy pronouncements, Abdul Kader fell over her grave, howling, "Ore Ma!" Morzina's cousin Alamgir had pierced a machete through his heart. The gurgling stream of blood covered Morzina's grave in red. While everyone tended to Abdul Kader's wounds, Alamgir threw the blade away and fled the scene. Out of fear of the knife or with the silent support of those on the scene or, perhaps, even complying with the norms of letting the killer flee or thinking that there must be some logical reason behind the killing and forgiving the person for it—all this played a role in how Alamgir was able to commit the murder publicly and escape.

Within a few days, the villagers' memories had dissolved into a haze. They couldn't remember who the murderer was. Even as Alamgir walked amongst them, the police and the people could not find the killer. As for Abdul Kader, he left this world without his loved ones knowing. Even though a copy of his files were available at the school's office, there was no way of notifying his village. There were no cell phones at the time, and the nearest landline was located far from the village. Moreover, there was no phone number listed in his files. Though the police had arrived to seize the body, his grave ended up beside Morzina's for practical reasons. There was no way to preserve the body, so they couldn't wait for his family to arrive. A murder case was filed, though no progress was ever made on the case.

Shortly after the incident, a relative came to the village and collected Abdul Kader's belongings and a few hundred takas from the school. He visited Abdul Kader's grave and gave Morzina's mother fifty takas to feed the poor. Though the story seemed to end there, for a long while, the mood of the village was clouded over. Young and old, wives and daughters, no one would leave their houses late at night alone to answer the call of nature. Even though everyone had said prayers for the salvation of Morzina and Abdul Kader's souls, their incorporeal spirits still haunted the village. Many began to say that Abdul Kader had wanted Morzina to sleep with him, and either he had set Morzina on fire or she had been forced to take her own life. Perhaps she thought this was the only way to save herself. Morzina's cousin Alamgir had somehow witnessed the scene, which prompted his murder of Abdul Kader. Those who believed this story celebrated Alamgir. But others said that God wouldn't tolerate such blatant propaganda against a pious man like Abdul Kader. Alamgir was a ruffian who had murdered Abdul Kader to exact revenge for the teacher beating him with a cane when he was in school because he had never learned his lessons.

If Fotae Bibi had still been alive, she could've found an answer to this mystery. Everyone used to say there were Jinns on her shoulder, and many of her prophecies had come true. She had been right that Abdul Khalek would die by falling from a tree. He himself had ridiculed the notion while clinging to the top of a tree. He was a favorite of the children for his climbing skills. It wasn't easy scaling trees full of thorns or stealing eggs from pigeon nests. Fotae Bibi had cursed Abdul Khalek publicly for killing the pigeons' offspring, saying that he would contract leprosy, that his hands and knees would go limp if he snatched a young one from its parents' bosom and he would die in agony. Kids did this all the time, however. They made slingshots from tree branches and attached erasers to them to shoot at birds' nests. They often killed birds with these contraptions, intentionally or not. In human culture, to kill is valiant; those who can kill more are honored more. Committing one or two murders is always considered a crime. But those who murder the murderer are honored even more.

When this story was being written, Alamgir's end was yet to come. Or perhaps the prophecy Fotae Bibi could see for him was unknown to us. Or perhaps the villagers were speechless out of fear. It isn't the murder itself but rather the audience, the witnesses who see the crime taking place, whose speech and accompanying speechlessness decide the possibility of another killing. Murder has been with us since ancient times. People do not kill just to snatch the victim's wealth. There's an aesthetic pleasure to it as well, a certain joy in the act. At times it becomes necessary to kill for one's nation or family or beliefs. The state's appointed executioners think of themselves as preventing more murders taking place, that if they do not assist the state in this murder, they themselves might be murdered one day.

Hasan has heard about eight Bangladeshis who were beheaded in Saudi Arabia. There was debate as to whether they were Bengali or Rohingya. One wonders what advantage the headless body would've had being Rohingya instead of Bengali. Perhaps the people of Bangladesh would be happy knowing it wasn't one of their own. The government would be relieved too. They would tread lightly, hoping to not provoke the Saudi Badshah, for his ire would lead to countless poor folk exiled in the deserts being unable to send back gold bars as remittances. The reserves in Bangladesh Bank would ebb if this financial flow were obstructed, and the means for sending four and a half billion takas to gain royal favor would tighten. Perhaps the bullion would quicken to life, like the chirping magic of the forty thieves. They would cross the borders of the real world and go over to the virtual universe.

Hasan had read an interview in the paper with the executioner of those eight men. How could a person cut off another person's head as if the person were merely an animal and able to keep food in their stomach? How comfortably they ladled the cooked portions of chicken and beef onto flatbread and put it in their mouths. Moreover, it is strictly forbidden to completely remove the heads of chickens and cows when they are beheaded and allow them to fall on the ground. When that happens, the animal isn't considered halal and cannot be eaten. Perhaps a reason for this practice is to avoid acting with complete barbarity or even to leave the door open to other possibilities. But since there aren't any limitations on eating the animals' flesh, what difference would the completeness of beheading make? We have always considered living animals as livestock. Only humans can stake a claim on food for humans. Our worth regarding each other depends on whether the other produces or kills our food for us.

It is still a matter of debate as to what is the best way to kill a person: beheading, death by firing squad, or hanging. And how much does it matter to the person given the death sentence? Even if he might have some say about what his last meal or who his last visitor might be, the state ultimately decides how he will die. One can't request death through lethal injection if he is directed to sit in the electric chair. Saddam Hussein had wanted to die by firing squad; perhaps he wanted to experience what he had made his enemies go through. But the state did not agree to his demands. The Saudi Badshah had said in a public meeting that he considered all his subjects as his children. To raise a hand against a Saudi national would mean raising it against his children. This was how he warned the non-Arabs. His children might kill as they please. Whoever comes from abroad to their kingdom is their slave. There is no barrier in their way; any transgression would lead to a beheading. We aren't all equal in Allah's world. Those born in the holy lands have more advantages.

Although Abdul Khalek wasn't able to express his wishes before he died, the angel of death was able to piece it together. Firstly, Abdul Khalek was ignorant in matters of the powers that be. The Kingdom then was fighting for religion, and their soldiers thought the Overlord had sent them to Earth to protect it. The inhabitants of the Kingdom who weren't interested in circumcision but worshipped the body instead of the abstract were a petty group of people standing in the way of the establishment of the Kingdom of God. These people would doubt the strength of His people. The doubts of these nonbelievers would spread in the Kingdom. Moreover, Abdul Khalek did not believe in the unseen. He had especially erred in not paying heed to Fotae Bibi's fortune-telling. He thought all this was just talk. He did not realize that Fotae Bibi, the old widow living alone on the eastern end of his yard, had no shortage of good relations with people from her own religion in the villages nearby. Especially to those who did not have mothers. She was a mother to many, a fairy godmother. She was a sister to those who didn't have sisters, a fairy godsister, perhaps? Even the elderly who had lived alone for so long that no one listened to them were embraced by Fotae Bibi.

Fortune tellers must have a mystical way about them that sets them apart from the others. This isn't true just for Rasputin and Rajneesh, but also for Fotae Bibi. People who came to her would offer their hand for a reading, anxious to know what the future held for them, unable to conceal their desires even as they had come over to ask the fortune teller about their intimate hopes and wishes. They lay down their troubles, they poured out all their longings. Fotae Bibi had mastered her own tactics in this regard. She could understand the minds of the young. She knew people didn't want much other than a good job or true love. Fotae Bibi knew there was pleasure in heartache.

Of course, Fotae Bibi had gotten herself in trouble once or twice. A youth from their village, Mohammad Hafez, had fallen in love with the daughter of an affluent man. Hafez too was from a well off family. He had been sent to the city to study at an Alia madrasah. He was about eighteen or nineteen years of age, and his looks weren't bad. His fair, reddened skin felt taut, as if a little poke would burst it open, releasing the juices within. His beard was yet to grow completely. The moustache over his lips and his beard was a thin line, untouched by the razor, and gave him an attractive demeanor.

Hafez had found himself at Fotae Bibi's mercy after falling for Rebecca Sultana, the daughter of Taizuddin. Even though they were from the same village, Hafez didn't realize the girl would bring him such heartache. She had just started high school. He hadn't yet spoken to her. But anticipating Rebecca's beauty had the whole village talking. Everyone was waiting until her thin body would grow beefy. For her breasts, waist, and buttocks to grow firm. She'd be quite a treat to look at. They would draw flattering versions of Rebecca in their heads. If any of those images had been recorded, it would have been a great work of art. But no one in the village painted. Artistic expression wasn't seen in a positive light. If one isn't able to breathe life into an image, one shouldn't draw it. This was a job set aside for Allah alone. No matter how many things humans invent, they can never create a living being, not even a fly. But Allah had created a world of pleasure and imagination in the opposite sex, a vast world of formless blobs, where no one can be reprimanded for exploring the extent of their desires. Hafez has noticed that the most beautiful and best qualities in human beings are neglected in human society, that these qualities in fact merit a reprimand. Yet one of Allah's names is *Khalek*—the one who creates, the architect who has decreed man to be bright in His colors, to exalt Him through the qualities He bestowed upon them. Humans are afraid to acquire many of these qualities, thinking that doing so would be inviting Allah's wrath. This was how the boundaries were maintained between earthly beings and the celestial, and thus the Lord's invisible universe was protected.

Hafez, however, does not understand why men would have to burn for drawing an image of this world. Drawing something and worshipping the image are two completely different aspects of consciousness and philosophy. It's only through color that man can really be known. We are a combination of an array of colors. Our bones, marrow, skin—they each possess different textures. Our piss and blood are different. Our nails and hair, the palm of our hands—we are a mixture of all these differences. Would a change of their color have animated us? Hafez had drawn an image of Rebecca Sultana in secret. She looked like Queen Razia Sultana of the Delhi Sultanate, chasing an enemy on horseback. The horse's front legs were raised. Razia's hard and delicate face were neck and neck with the horse's mane and her sword. Hafez had drawn her in the style of an equestrian fairy, whose speed and beauty rushes her toward an unknown world. Perhaps the mare he had drawn was influenced by something he saw in Rebecca. He wanted to stand beside an exhausted Razia like her lover Malik Altunia. He thought this was the life, to run free on a fairy-like horse, to bring walnuts and dates out of your pocket to replenish your-self. The horse's skin would act as a blade clashing against the ocean's sand, a dazzling sight across the universe. But no matter what human imagination summons, angels from heaven do not come down to earth. Rebecca and Hafez's story could've ended before it began, for it was not the custom in the village for boys and girls to have a relation-ship. Moreover, Rebecca's family did not want their daughter to wed Hafez. The stricter they were, the deeper Hafez's love became. In the end, unable to find a solution, Hafez had gone to see Fotae Bibi.

The fortune teller told him, "You must go to the cemetery on the night of a new moon, cut the fingers off a bastard child and bring the bone to me. I will make you an amulet from that bone, which you must wear at the waist and submerge yourself in the river to chant some mantras at night. Only then will Rebecca come to you."

It was far easier to prepare a grave in the earth or sacrifice one's life in war than to wander into the cemetery in the dark of night. And to bring oneself to cut the finger bones of a dead bastard child—impossible even for a fiend with Genghis Khan's nature. But as the days went by, Hafez became more and more frail, his infatuation taking the form of an illness. His mother tried all sorts of charms to no avail. Then an unexpected incident occurred. Hazera, the daughter of Osimuddir, gave birth to a bastard child. Even though she had been married seven months before, her in-laws did not believe the child was their son's. They accused Hazera of already being pregnant before the marriage, saying that her parents knew this and had married her off in a rush. The villagers had seen other children born in the seventh month of pregnancy and accepted them without alarm, but no one wanted to give Hazera the benefit of the doubt. They said that Hazera was of a questionable character and had flirted with others before her marriage. An elder in the village complained that when she yawned she would raise her arms. "Just a ploy to show off her tits to men!"

Six days after Hazera's allegedly bastard child was born, it died. Before its fate could be written, it had rejected the Earth. Perhaps it had asked the Lord to take it up to the heavens like Jesus since it had no father and no one wanted the responsibility. Since there was no fate written for him, he truly belonged to the Lord. The mere dust of His empire. The Lord must have heard him, the innocent child growing in the mother's womb that no one on earth had any use for, except Hafez, who needed the child's finger bone to win his beloved.

Hafez followed all of Fotae Bibi's instructions. On a night of the new moon in winter, he had gone down to the river, immersing himself unclothed to pray, the amulet containing the dead child's bones hanging around his waist. Even though he was resorting to an evil force, Hafez had no other way to overcome the knots the Lord's men had wrought to obstruct his path. What did Hafez want from Varuna, the god of the seas? What did he want from Shiva, the lord of destruction? That he would break free of all the rules of the earth. A human child melting with the ashes is blending into the water to meet his desires. The girl on the other side of the village who had fallen asleep before finishing her schoolwork—did she ever know that a river in its fervent desire to meet with the sea had gone dry in the middle of the road?

Hafez's story could end here. But Fotae Bibi's prophecies were never wrong. Hafez came down with deadly pneumonia after his night's worship, cutting his life short within seven days. News of his fate spread through the roads and the fields, where the story of their love had already been a topic of discussion. The village poet, Akkas, had even written a poem that he recited in the market and had printed in a city newspaper. He sold each performance of the poem for eight annas. Others questioned Rebecca's character, calling her a witch. A boy like Hafez, they said, wasn't born once in seven generations. What did Hafez lack, for her not to return his love? What did his father lack, for that matter? Meanwhile, Rebecca's father, after rejecting the proposal of marriage put to his family, was annoyed by the ill-founded stories about his daughter. He saw it as a mark of dishonor, he thought it would've been better to not have a daughter like her.

Whatever stories were told, Hafez could not be saved. After suffering frequent fits and weeping, he left the world for the heavens. A short while before that happened, Rebecca announced, despite public embarrassment, that she would marry only Hafez. That he was her husband, Allah had blessed their union. Even though Hafez was in no state to marry her now and her father wouldn't agree to it either, Rebecca too fell into intense crying fits that left him no choice. Although they did not have a wedding, on the day of his death, Rebecca appeared at his house in a bullock cart, dressed as a bride, accompanied by her grandmother. These theatrics made people far more curious. After Hafez's death, Rebecca maintained that as his wife, his parents' house was her rightful place. Even though Hafez's parents blamed her for their son's death, they grew to be fond of her, and Rebecca spent the rest of her days in their house, serving her "in-laws." Hafez's parents recompensed her by leaving Hafez's inheritance in her name, though she saw no value in it. That house, where now only a jungle surrounds the foundation, is known to be haunted. Hafez's father had no other children, and since Rebecca never remarried, the house went to ruin. She did not live very long after the passing of her in-laws. Perhaps with the ghosts in the house, she too had withered away.

The story of Hafez and Rebecca became part of the village's mythos, contributing to Fotae Bibi's mystique. As for Abdul Khalek, the subject of his fate did not come up in Hasan's dream. Nevertheless, it was sealed in the innumerable inevitabilities of destiny. Hasan can't deny the existence of fate. What else could one blame for the countless births and deaths of human beings? If only there was a way to call God and Fate by the same name, he thought.

Abdul Khalek might have been a little dumb, but he could adapt to the intricacies of the village. Just as Fotae Bibi had been counting the fortunes of those around her for as long as anyone could remember, Abdul Khalek was hanging from a wobbly branch of a date palm tree like a bat to substantiate those lies. Bibi Fotae had foretold, *Khalek will die falling off a tree.* On November 24, 1971, the morning was clear. The heat had sweetened with the coming of winter. The brief cold was comforting. Though it was not yet the season for date palm juice, trees were being shaved to make climbing easier. Abdul Khalek had already stuck his tongue against the bark to taste the sweetness. He never missed an opportunity to climb up a tree. But he didn't know that, with gravity, no matter how far someone goes away from the earth, one day they'd have to return to it.

Everyone else had fled that day when they heard that the Pakistani military was arriving. But Abdul Khalek did not fear the military. This is why it is proper to teach fear as part of our education. Only when we are able to inculcate fear at home and beyond are we educating our people well, for success arrives with fear. Fear helps keep us alive. Abdul Khalek's heart was empty of fear; people like him can't protect themselves in this world or the next. Abdul Khalek couldn't save himself from a Pakistani solder, hell-bent on preserving his holy land. It was clear that his stupidity could not be explained away as a possible collaboration with the occupiers. Since he hadn't directly been a martyr and his name wasn't listed with those that were sent back from India, it wasn't possible to find out his whereabouts. Moreover, he didn't have any relatives who could benefit from his martyrdom.

Afterward, Abu Taleb discovered the body first. Abu Taleb had disappeared before the war began. Everyone said he had joined one of the Rajakar forces. The Pakistani military brought him with them during this operation. As they were leaving the houses of the village in flames, Abu Taleb noticed Abdul Khalek's body lying on the ground beneath the tree. Brain matter had spilled out of his nose and mouth. His head had been smacked open. A bullet had gone through his shoulder and out his chest. When the Pakistani military first arrived, Abu Taleb had ordered Abdul Khalek to welcome them by climbing up the largest tree in the village. It was only for a little fun, but Abdul Khalek paid dearly for it. The soldiers had clapped in joy at seeing him climb the tree. As a reward they pulled out a rifle and shot him in the shoulder, as if it was a hunting celebration.

Even though Abdul Mottaleb had barred Abdul Khalek from climbing trees, in the end, Fotae Bibi's prophecy rang true. The snake *did* bite the snake charmer to death.

Saving Grace

asan is at his in-laws'. Before his time in prison, he had barely visited them, let alone stayed for days. Their company was an alien prospect to him, full of expected rituals and saccharine affections. It was all for show; they *had* to do it. He knows at the back of his mind that they do not like him much.

Since arriving at their home, he has seen Fariha only briefly. Other than making an occasional comment in front of the family, she does not seem to be in the mood to talk.

One day, when he is lying in bed, Fariha comes over, acting like her normal self, although Hasan doesn't feel at peace.

"You're thinner. You haven't eaten properly for many days," she says.

Hasan says, "You're mad at me. Aren't you, Ria, truly?"

Before, there was a time when a wife would only enter her husband's room when all the housework was finished and her in-laws were in bed. That was the custom among rich and poor, educated and illiterate, whether it was a communal, joint, or nuclear family. It wasn't as it is now with households living in five-story buildings, where one couldn't separate themselves from others even if they wanted to. If someone was angry, there was nothing one could do except cry in bed or to one side. The intricacies of such relationships perhaps affect the intensity of the union.

At dinner, his father-in-law says, "How are things going, young man? My daughter is greatly disturbed by everything that happened. My advice is to let it be. These things happen. What is the point of talking about it? Danger will come when it will come."

Fariha's tummy is enlarged. Their future—their lives will center on it. Alone with her in his room, Hasan wants dearly to put his ears on her belly to hear their child's beating heart. Though her belly has grown larger than her breasts and buttocks, her beauty hasn't dimmed at all. Nevertheless, Hasan restrains himself. Anything might happen at this stage of pregnancy.

Fariha says, "You can do whatever you feel like doing. This is the last time."

Hasan is surprised. "The last time?"

"No point in you knowing our child."

Hasan tries to draw Fariha into his arms, but she screams. "Don't touch me! Never! Go to your street women. Your hands are dirty, you're a dirty man."

"Listen to me. Did you truly believe them? Is this where our relationship has gone? What have I done that you are acting like this!"

"I don't care. Never touch me again. Stay where you are. You know how I am."

It has come true, what Hasan feared. At another time, it wouldn't have hurt him, but today he is feeling sorry for himself and the dilemma he has gotten himself into. Their child will be born soon. If something happens to Fariha now, he will blame himself.

He knew she might react this way. But he had tried to think positively. If one's family isn't supportive in one's time of need, where would one go? Men and women are two separate species. They come from different families and different environments to cohabit under the same roof in one bed. Their being together results in children making the leap from an invisible world to this one. One doesn't need to have love and trust for this to happen. When a flower blooms, a bee goes to and from it bearing pollen; a relationship is built which can go against their will as well. The natural world does not always align with the world as we imagine it to be. People are bitten by snakes and dogs on the streets or attacked by tigers and buffalos in rural places, but only when the police set upon them does it become a humiliation for the entire lot. How was it his fault that the police had caught him? Was it his fault that he didn't want to sleep with the girls who approached him in the street? How could he make Fariha understand this?

At another time, Hasan would've made more effort to understand Fariha's moods. Today he isn't feeling it. He thinks a part of his life has ended. When a wife loses trust, there is no meaning left in the marriage. Some couples go on to sleep with others, but that's a different thing. There's no question of trust there, only the pretense of trust. But if one is subjected to suspicion without having transgressed with another woman, then there is nothing left in the relationship. Hasan does not want to live like this with Fariha.

"Ria, did you really think the police's accusations were true? That I was caught red-handed doing things with street girls?"

"Of course not, you're too pious! You have destroyed my life. You act innocent, thinking no one knows what you've been up to all this while. If you were going to do this, why did you marry me in the first place?"

"What did I do? Was this my fault? Accidents happen in the streets. People die in the streets. Are they responsible for their own deaths? Do hurricanes and earthquakes come announced?"

"Leave it, I can't listen to your lecture anymore. You go your own way; give me my freedom. I can't live my life like this. How will I show my face to my friends now?"

When Fariha is angry with him, she addresses him in a mocking tone of formality. Perhaps all wives do that. The wife has the right to call her husband by all sorts of names.

Hasan has no strength in him. It wouldn't be wise to provoke her, anyway. She has truly been hurt, any woman would be in her situation. When a woman's husband is desired by other women, she might perversely take pride in the matter, but when her husband desires other women, she has no place to stand. One could wave it aside as a temporary mistake if it happens in secret, but when it is public knowledge, the scars never leave their minds. People love drilling holes into others. There's no sugarcoating available at that moment.

Abruptly, Fariha turns cheerful. Hasan wipes the tears from her eyes. She pulls his hands over her chest, touches his fingers with her lips, then sucks them between her lips.

He says, "Are you angry with me?" The stone that had been pressing on him falls from his chest. The rain that had been flowing over him is instantly extinguished. Tiredness and depression disappear—he realizes that his anxiety over Fariha's reaction was the cause for the pressure on his mind. Now he has no sadness, no fatigue. If Fariha forgives him and takes the matter easily, what else is there for him to worry about? *I can never leave Fariha, I must stay with her at all times, carry our future child on my shoulders.*

They caress each other for a long time.

Afterward, in a deep slumber, Hasan begins to hallucinate. He has had these moments before and thought of going to see a doctor about it, then reassured himself that it was nothing. Also that it wasn't unnatural for him to experience this now, after what he had gone through. He often feels as if an evil force was always destroying the path he was taking toward his goals. Is he responsible for it? However one saw life, not everyone had the capacity to weather difficulties. People make mistake upon mistake quite unaware of their role in it. Now he understands that he shouldn't have been curious about the girls in the street that night. The tragedy that has befallen him, how will he come out of it? He should've thought of his wife, thought of their unborn child. Hasan realizes that man is put on earth to cater to his partner's happiness and their child's future. All the work he does is for the safety of these two. That is the meaning of production.

Hasan always returns to his adolescence in his dreams. A winter morning with a fog-ridden river, where the water turns into vapor, which mixes with the sky. Even though the sun stands his ground, nothing can be seen clearly in the fog. Through the trees and mustard fields at the back of the house, a girl is running toward him with a flag in her hand.

The girl says, "Why are you looking at me like this? I feel shy when you do that." She wears her saree in a knot, without a blouse and petticoat. Of course, back then in the village, no one would wear such things. They had never seen brassieres. The age of lingerie hadn't yet arrived. Hasan wonders, so much thought has gone into women, so much poetry.

The girl with the flag is none other than Morzina, coming toward his house. She is seated in a bullock cart dressed as a bride, surrounded by trumpeters and other vehicles dressed for celebration. Yet he remembers that Morzina had died in a fire at her home, that Moulavi Abdul Kader been knifed while they were laying her in her grave. Behind the tree in his dream, a group of childhood friends are busy with an absurd game of adulthood, playing at marriage, love, and sex, childbirth and child-rearing, the blooming of relations. One of them is Morzina, trying to wake him with light taps, saying, "Will you just sleep or help the girl? I don't get a moment's respite while you sleep at home like Kumbhakarna." Truly, he feels like there is a young child on his lap looking at him, dangling its feet, making noises as if wanting to say something. Its body had turned red in various places in proximity to the fire. Then he remembers that they have come here to play, that they are still children themselves playing pretend. How could their child be real? Would the people in his village accept their child? Perhaps his father would scold him, his mother too. Suddenly Morzina begins to cry, wetting the bed. Children do not like lying in wet beds. They have greater sensitivity; their soft bodies are quite delicate. The sound of the twigs, the song of the wind, the tunes of the river, the calls of the birds—they could differentiate between them all. Morzina is cooking by the river on a steep bank. Suddenly she screams, "Fire, fire! Look how much my body has burned!" Hasan places his hands on her, but as soon as he does, someone shoves him away.

Hasan senses that Fariha is awake. She had pushed his hand aside when it travelled over the border between them in his sleep. She is crying. The tears of women could be understood as a sign that an understanding is in the offing. When women lose their strength, when they want to end hostilities and see that they won't get any more from their companion's reactions, they bring out their tears as weapons.

The degree and severity of the crying depends on the situation and the women.

As soon as Hasan touches Fariha, she begins to cry more loudly. "You can never touch me again the rest of your life. You've lost the right."

Hasan tries to stay calm. "Look, I may be the one who made the mistake. But the child in your belly is innocent. Why are you punishing the child? I won't touch you anymore. It will be as you want it to be."

"I have no wish to listen to anything you say. Since the man I wanted to spend the rest of my life with acts like this, I have no concerns about what will come or not. I've understood that any child I give birth to will have to live in this world of betrayal. It will also have to go through the torment I've gone through. And if it's a boy, it will grow up to be like you. I don't want my son to be like you. Let him stay within the contours of my body."

Hasan is frightened by her words. He knew she'd had some emotional difficulties and suicidal thoughts. When she is well, there isn't a better wife than her, but when she is upset, the ugliness inside her creeps out. Hasan has thought of splitting up with her but didn't, because he didn't want to bring further pain to the girl. What if she acted rashly and hurt herself? And Hasan loves Fariha—that is the most important factor. He loves her, truly. After they were married, he realized he had married the right girl. The Lord had created them as a pair up in heaven, a belief that led Hasan to prioritize the marriage even before love developed. Marital discord is easier to handle if there is love after marriage. Although love cannot be long-lasting, the warmth it gives while it does is what we know as love. Compassion and duty take their place soon after, laying the foundation for the couple's future. But if love exists before the marriage, it begins to break up after, when the couple discovers each other's mysteries or begins to understand one another. Hasan used to think that a majority of the love-marriages ended in unhappiness. But is there really much difference between marrying who you're in love with and who your parents select for you? Has anyone claimed that the wives of Vidyasagar or Rabindranath weren't good enough because they didn't have the acumen for business or work? At least in marriages arranged by the family, there is someone to blame. When one marries of their own accord, there is no one but themselves to point fingers at. Of course, now people are choosing their own mates from their schools, colleges, or workplaces. Hasan finds it hard to say whether this is good or bad. Regardless of what he thinks, the hypothesis does not ring true in his case. His arranged marriage hasn't been able to sidestep the present crisis.

A few days after their wedding, Hasan had realized that when Fariha wanted to hurt somebody, she would abuse herself. At times, this took the form of physical self-harm. She would cut herself until she was bloody. If she felt someone had shown contempt for her, she would get angry, then break things in the house and cry fervently. She wouldn't come back to normal until she had expended all of her strength expressing herself. She would even go without eating for days. His in-laws knew about this and thought it would go away after marriage, that the love and adoration of her husband would make it go away. They had consulted a doctor in secret as well. He had given them the same advice.

A certain physiological problem did go away after they married. Fariha used to experience excruciating physical discomfort during menstruation. Doctors call this dysmenorrhea. Sometimes it affects women so much so that they cannot go to school or work, disrupting the regularity of their lives. While many women experience pain during their periods, dysmenorrhea can be due to mental stress, ovarian cysts, illness, or other causes. Conventional wisdom is that the pain goes away after marriage. It worked like magic in Fariha's case. However, she became more susceptible to sadness. It would creep up on her for little to no reason. Hasan had experienced such feelings himself and recognizes them when they befall him. But instead of coming up with a solution, he often leads himself toward further complications of thought that extend his unhappiness. He considers this a consequence of his sensitivity. Society is rotting away. No one is doing what they are supposed to do; everyone is suffering, angry, hurt, and engulfed in depression.

After being released from detention, Hasan decided to be only attentive toward his wife and the future of his child. Everyone's better off thinking for themselves. He wasn't going to be a king or emperor. He'd move aside the moment any trouble arose. He had learned the hard way the consequences of standing in the way of the storm.

Hasan had talked to a psychiatrist friend about Fariha behind her back. He said, "She's quite nice, she'll give you everything, but when she is suspicious of you, she could take away your life." Three months into their marriage she had tried to knife him with a boti. Was this why the goddesses Durga and Kali were depicted with swords? Perhaps this iconography was a result of male experience. She didn't do it again, but Hasan had become cautious. He wouldn't talk to his female friends. Fariha would act like nothing was wrong, but the anger remained within her. Like fire stamped beneath the ashes, it wasn't completely extinguished.

His doctor friend had said this was not that big of a problem. Most women were similar, his own wife acted in this way. Medical science was only there to stifle the illness long enough for us to accept that there was no solution available. Human life goes by so fast, perhaps death is the only solution. Hasan did not like the doctor's words. Was there no point to his field of study, then?

The doctor also suggested that Fariha had body dysmorphic disorder, even though he had never met her. Women have it more than men, he said. Their insecurities about their body are severe enough to make them ill. They think their partners will be attracted to others because their own looks, they perceive, are not attractive. The way the doctor spoke about it, even Hasan had begun to feel insecure and depressed.

If not for being in prison and now the aftermath, Hasan probably would not have thought about all this. No one knows when the apocalypse will arrive in their lives, though he senses now that it is coming for him. It would have been better to die before. But there are moments in life when it isn't possible to take the antidote beforehand. Like now, for instance, he feels it would've been better to not come here, that he and Fariha would have been better off not having a child. They should've separated. He shouldn't have acted the way he did with the police. Why did he give the street girls money anyway? He didn't have the answers. At any rate, he'd lost so much. Now he wonders how he'll face the situation in front of him.

Fariha is in the bathroom. He can hear the shower running. At first, he is not alarmed. There's nothing unusual about going to the restroom at night, and it isn't strange to spend a long time inside. But the shower doesn't stop. Fariha is still in the bathroom. She has locked the door as well. Though winter hasn't started, the cold water would be freezing at night. Hasan thinks, perhaps she is angry at me, trying to get back at me by hurting herself. Hasan thinks of the movie *Psycho*, perhaps because of the shower scene. His chest trembles.

"Ria, open the door!" Hasan shouts. "What are you doing? Have you gone mad? Come out." He hears nothing but groans from inside.

Hasan pushes hard against the door. It doesn't move. He hears crying sounds and sits down. Fariha's parents come in from the other room. With Hasan, they manage to break down the bathroom door.

Fariha is lying on the bathroom floor. Her clothes are in disarray. The cold water from the shower is splashing against her face. She is making noises like an injured animal. The water is tinged with red.

Hasan has a fear of blood. They call it hemophobia in the medical field. He did not remember how he developed this phobia. Doctors say that it could be genetic. What one fears, one has to carry within one-self. The body's vigor gives one courage, it becomes the subject of jealousy and joy—one surely would be depressed at the thought of it being rendered immobile.

We pass down to our progeny what we inherit from our ancestors. What else could this be other than the sum of the earth's elements? When blood, flesh, and feces come out of our bodies, they cause fear and disgust. Fortunately, two-thirds of the people in the world do not suffer from hemophobia, and even those who do have it in varying degrees. In some, it's latent and never comes up.

Hasan has never faced such a frightening situation before. There was the time he had seen Moulavi Abdul Kader knifed in the back. Everyone in the village, old and young, had been at the cemetery to attend Morzina's burial. As women weren't allowed to attend the funeral, they crowded in front of their houses to watch the procession. Many wiped tears with their clothes, while others cursed under their breath. Hasan had quite the view that day, seeing Abdul Kader's blood gurgle up like that of a sacrificial animal, how it jettisoned out of the body and dried upon contact with the earth and wind. In a few months, the blood would be replaced by a watery stain on the ground. And though it might be washed away in the rain and sun, the stain within the heart would stay forever.

Once, there had been a deadly incident in the village. Hasan was returning from a relative's house, walking on the road past the fields. The sun hadn't completely set yet and was waiting in the broad fields with its parting yellow. One or two men were running around in great distress, flailing, screaming, sighing. A crowd was gathered nearby.

When someone asked what was going on, the sighing men said, "Habil Paramanik has been murdered in the field."

Hasan's father pushed into the crowd, Hasan followed behind him. A tall, broad man was sprawled motionless on the ground, encircled by the men. His arms were splayed out, his feet spread apart as if he was sleeping. His mouth and eyes were wide open. Blood ran down his mouth and nose, much of it from the ears. The bullet had penetrated beside his ear; some brain matter had been shot out too. The left side of his head was fully drenched in blood.

Red ants were accumulating around the blood. No one had touched the body, no one from his family had arrived. Who had killed him? Everyone knew, but no one was saying the name. Instead they were muttering to themselves. How could men be so cruel? Habil did not know one shouldn't fool around with someone who had a gun. He thought he had the right to joke with his friend. But he didn't have any rights with the gun. The gun could only kill. It was for the best to stay away from those who had predatory sensibilities, who were proud to mark lifeless bodies as their own.

Habil had said to his friend, "It doesn't look like your gun can kill anyone. BB guns for killing birds are bigger than that." He did not know that the gun's size had nothing to do with its power. The friend had said, "Let's test it then." With that, he aimed it at Habil's head. Though Habil was a little frightened, he thought they were still joking for fun. But whatever he might have wanted to say, he wasn't able to. His head gave a jerk, and he fell to the ground.

Everyone was afraid of touching the body. Some said they should wait for the police to arrive, it wouldn't be wise to leave their hand prints. Hasan's father covered the dead man's body with his shawl. Usually no one dares to do this when someone dies in an accident. The police would want to know who the owner of the shawl was. Where had it come from? Who put it on them? The shawl's owner could be implicated. Even the murderer whose bullet had perforated the dead man's body might be acquitted without a witness, but the shawl's owner, if caught red-handed, would be punished until the end of time.

The image of red ants helplessly stuck in a stream of blood had quite the effect on young Hasan's mind. Blood is red in every person, in every sacrificial cow, in many of the animals who roam the land on four legs or two. If all their blood were shed at once, the roads and footpaths, rice fields and mountains and hills, deserts and seas would all be enveloped by this red. Red is the deepest light wave. It attracts our attention more than any other color. It's the color of fire, which is accompanied by oxygen. One cannot burn without it. When the strength of this red is magnified, it becomes infrared. Rabindranath would've called it Upstream Red. Not only is it impressionable, but it calls up from us the emotions of rebellion. This is why people become frightened looking at red. It can sweep everything away. It brings us back to our past. The color rocks our blood along with heat, energy, anger, and love. A little of it creates fear and longing.

Hasan had fainted that day at the sight of red. He couldn't remember anything afterward. He had a fever, he was trembling in fear. They had cured him for the time being with the help of the pirs and fakirs. But the color of blood remained perennially a cause for fear. A doctor told him he had to overcome the fear by looking frequently at blood. At first, his family would strategically get him to help with killing chickens at home. He would hold the animal's feet while someone slashed the neck in two, although not all the way through. That was forbidden. The Lord had set down rules about murder after He had created the world. To kill due to anger, jealousy, or hatred is a great sin, but killing in His name is acceptable. When one kills an animal in His name, the Lord takes responsibility for it. He takes in the soul of the animal and provides us with another life, for He knows everyone will return to Him one day.

Hasan's head shakes as he sees the water from the shower mixing with the red of blood. His last refuge—his wife, his family, his future—is collapsing before his eyes. His unborn child—he cannot bear the distress. After the humiliation of the night, he only thinks of escape, of running away that very night or perhaps returning to the custody of the police. He will go to the station and hit someone, because their actions that day have had grave consequences in his life. Society has found him unclean and is unwilling to entertain him. Before he can do anything, Hasan faints.

In the end, it isn't possible to save their child. Due to excessive bleeding and their slowness in getting to the hospital, the child is dead by the time Fariha gives birth. Her own hold on life is uncertain too, afflicted as she is with grief, depression, and pneumonia. For the first few days after going to hospital, she doesn't recognize anybody. The doctor says she had eclampsia, brought on by extreme mental stress. She has breathing problems, as well as fits. Fariha is floating in a rudderless, sinking ship.

Hasan is admitted to a rehabilitation center. Bilu thinks Hasan is on leave, that the Editor sent him away to rest. She knows that Fariha is supposed to give birth soon, and the timing confuses her. Bilu has been thinking of getting in touch to see how Hasan is doing, whether her foolish friend had gotten himself in trouble again. Although he was born with quite the intelligence, it has rendered him unfit to live in this world. He spends his days dreaming of another world. Bilu herself has been going through a stressful time. She feels like there are many things in life one can't decide on one's own. This includes relationships that are meant to last a lifetime. Just as one can't choose one's parents or siblings, we can't choose our children or in-laws.

Bilu's grandmother used to say women were created from the ribs of men. Bilu would say, "Grandma! A man can have multiple wives or leave one wife for another. The wife can also leave her husband to have a new husband."

Her grandmother wasn't too keen on these complicated accounts. "Multiple wives can be born of a single rib."

"I understand that," Bilu would say. "But how could one person be created from two or three ribs? Those who have multiple husbands on earth, where would they go?"

Her grandmother would say, "You've become quite the pundit, I see. The Creator does not do justice to what your little brain comes up with."

Bilu considers the inevitable way a man and a woman, though strangers, could live together, despite the fragility of their relationship.

If there isn't a change in how humans procreate, why should there be any change in how relationships between men and women are forged? Men had constructed this arrangement, she suspects. They had brought women to serve them. From their parents' house to their in-laws' house—there was no life outside of this for women, spending their whole lives inside the four walls of their homes with children and grandchildren. The day her parents handed her to a man, their race to unearth each other's mysteries would begin, their lives of love and disgust would start. None of this is any different today. As more women are financially self-sufficient, many marriages are breaking up. In many countries, the custom of marriage itself is endangered. Couples have children and spend years together before thinking of marrying; at that stage, they may question the need to marry at all. But marriage is also important to determine inheritance in the eyes of the state. If human beings didn't have children and there wasn't any system of inheritance, marriage wouldn't be needed to shield the division between the sexes.

Now Bilu is almost twenty-eight. If she were like Rabindranath's or Nazrul's wife, she would have been married thirteen years ago. Of course, a marriage of this nature would be considered wrong today, bearing in mind women's health and the law. There's also the fact that one can take better care of one's children when one is older. But Bilu has also doubted herself and been a victim of romanticism. If only she had the luck of those girls! If Rabindranath, Nazrul, or Vidyasagar had proposed to marry her, would she have cared about her age? As for their majestic wives, they didn't have to look for news to report for the newspaper or find their own husbands. They followed the advice of their grandparents and married men their father's age—obviously they made choices shaped by their time.

Bilu goes to the rehabilitation center in Shyamoli after receiving a call from there. She can't believe that so much has happened in such a short while. She hadn't even known there was an institution of this sort in the city. People don't like keeping tabs on hospitals and cemeteries unless there's a personal need. That's how the buildings of the city are erected, to stay out of each other's business. The mental hospitals aren't any different, built as securely as a prison, as if those dwelling within might burst out and attack others in due time.

Hasan is lying on a metal bed. His legs are brought up to his chest. Even though this is a private mental hospital, patients wear a uniform of a specific color so that they can be identified as such. Patients were usually admitted after the proper documentation was presented, but many families gave false information and never returned for their loved ones. The hospital authorities regularly had to deal with such problems. Corruption was prevalent here as well, as it was in other hospitals. Patients weren't treated properly in the absence of their relatives.

Bilu quickly finds out that, after the incidents of that night, Hasan hasn't returned to his normal mental state. Though he has recovered his senses, he remains silent and isn't talking at all. Perhaps Fariha's hospital stay and the death of their unborn child—all this has led to his ruin. The most shocking thing they told her was that Fariha's father was getting divorce papers ready.

What had happened that night when he was returning home from the office? Bilu wonders. Just because he reacted to the police, he has gone through such misfortune.

Bilu sits beside Hasan. He has his face turned toward the wall. He is hard to recognize with his beard. Bilu leans toward him and asks, "Do you recognize me, philosopher Abdul Hasan? Apparently you have gone mad? You dream of change with this soul of a mouse!"

Hasan looks back at her and smiles a little.

She tries to get as much information about him from the doctor making his rounds. From his report, she understands that Hasan had these symptoms a long while back; many do. That the unexpected incident had brought him to this state. With proper treatment, he could recover completely, though if he wasn't cautious, it could show up again.

After the doctor moves on, the nurse on duty asks Bilu if she knew of these problems before their marriage.

Bilu says she did. Then she looks at the nurse and gives her a mischievous smile.

Acknowledgments

I would like to thank my wife and children for their relentless support. I have had the pleasure of working with many bright editors, writers and journalists over the years, and I thank them all for their important suggestions and advice. My editors at Gaudy Boy—Jee Leong Koh, Kimberley Lim and Yu-Mei Balasingamchow—did tremendous work on this novel, and I am grateful for their insight and for making sure *Memorial Club* sees the light of day! I would also like to thank the people at Bhorer Kagoj Press for championing the book in its original publication in Bangla. Jonathan McAloon, Rafee Shaams, Shyamal Dutta, Salek Nasir Uddin and many others have read the work and given helpful suggestions. Lastly, I am perennially in debt to my hometown of Pabna, where I spent much of my childhood. Without those memories, this novel would not have been possible.

About the Author

Mozid Mahmud is a poet, essayist, and novelist based in Dhaka, Bangladesh. Born in Pabna and educated at the University of Dhaka, he is recognized as a major Bangladeshi poet of the 1980s. He is the author of more than fifty titles, some of which include *Mahfuzamongol* (1989), *Toward the Pasture* (1995), *The Birth of the Maternity Clinic* (2006), and *Rabindranath's Travelogues* (2010). He worked as a journalist for various dailies and news organizations before setting up his own nonprofit organization to work for social advancement causes. A noted scholar on Kazi Nazrul Islam, he was awarded the Rabindra-Nazrul Literary Prize in 2006, the National Press Club Award in 2008, and the Bengali

Writers' Honors in London in 2010. Recently, his fiction and essays have appeared in *Singapore Unbound, Provenance Journal, Indian Quarterly, Borderless,* and *adda.* Many of his works have been translated into English, Chinese, Hindi, and French. *Memorial Club* is his debut novel.

From the Latin *gaudium*, meaning "joy," Gaudy Boy publishes books that delight readers with the various powers of art. The name is taken from the poem "Gaudy Turnout," by Singaporean poet Arthur Yap, about his time abroad in Leeds, the United Kingdom. Similarly inspired by such diasporic wanderings and migrations, Gaudy Boy brings literary works by authors of Asian heritage to the attention of an American audience and beyond. Established in 2018 as the imprint of the New York City–based literary nonprofit Singapore Unbound, we publish poetry, fiction, and literary nonfiction.

Visit our website at www.singaporeunbound.org/gaudyboy.

Winners of the Gaudy Boy Poetry Book Prize

Interrogation Records: Poems
by Jeddie Sophronius

Waking Up to the Pattern Left by a Snail Overnight: Poems
by Jim Pascual Agustin

Time Regime: Poems
by Jhani Randhawa

Object Permanence: Poems
by Nica Bengzon

Play for Time: Poems
by Paula Mendoza

Autobiography of Horse: A Poem
by Jenifer Sang Eun Park

The Experiment of the Tropics: Poems
by Lawrence Lacambra Ypil

Fiction and Nonfiction

The Way You Want to Be Loved: Stories
by Aruni Kashyap

Lovelier, Lonelier: A Novel
by Daryl Qilin Yam

Bengal Hound: A Novel
by Rahad Abir

The Infinite Library and Other Stories
by Victor Fernando R. Ocampo

The Sweetest Fruits: A Novel
by Monique Truong

And the Walls Come Crumbling Down
by Tania De Rozario

The Foley Artist: Stories
by Ricco Villanueva Siasoco

Malay Sketches: Stories
by Alfian Sa'at

Other Series

New Singapore Poetries
edited by Marylyn Tan and Jee Leong Koh

Suspect: Volume 1, Year 1
edited by Jee Leong Koh

From Gaudy Boy Translates

Picking off new shoots will not stop the spring:
Witness Poems and Essays from Burma/Myanmar 1988–2021
edited by Ko Ko Thett and Brian Haman

Amanat: Women's Writing from Kazakhstan
edited by Zaure Batayeva and Shelley Fairweather-Vega

Ulirát: Best Contemporary Stories in Translation from the Philippines
edited by Tilde Acuña, John Bengan, Daryll Delgado, Amado Anthony G.
Mendoza III, and Kristine Ong Muslim

Books by our other imprint, Bench Press

Sample and Loop: A Simple History of Singaporeans in America
by Jee Leong Koh

Snow at 5 PM: Translations of an Insignificant Japanese Poet
by Jee Leong Koh

Seven Studies for a Self-Portrait: Poems
by Jee Leong Koh

Equal to the Earth: Poems
by Jee Leong Koh

Lightly in the Good of Day: Poems
by Bob Hart

Try to Have Your Writing Make Sense:
The Quintessential PFFA Anthology: Poems
edited by Donna Smith and Howard Miller

www.ingramcontent.com/pod-product-compliance
Lightning Source LLC
Chambersburg PA
CBHW021718190726
48289CB00008B/2584